by P. L. Travers

MARY POPPINS

MARY POPPINS COMES BACK

MARY POPPINS OPENS THE DOOR

MARY POPPINS IN THE PARK

MARY POPPINS FROM A TO Z

MARY POPPINS IN THE KITCHEN
A Cookery Book with a Story

A day in the park

MARY POPPINS
POPPINS
OPENS THE DOOR

By P. L. Travers

Illustrated by Mary Shepard *and* Agnes Sims

HOUGHTON MIFFLIN HARCOURT
Boston   New York

TO KATHARINE CORNELL

www.hmhco.com

The text of this book is set in Arno Pro.
The display type is set in Monster Fiesta.

The Library of Congress has cataloged the hardcover edition as follows:
Travers, P. L., 1899–1996.
Mary Poppins opens the door/P. L. Travers; illustrated by Mary Shepard.
p. cm.
Summary: Mary Poppins returns to the Banks family in a rocket and involves the Banks
children in more magical adventures, including those with Peppermint Horses, the
Marble Boy, and the Cat That Looked at the King.
[1. Fantasy.]
I. Shepard, Mary, 1909–2000. ill. II. Sims, Agnes. III. Title.
PZ7.T689Mat10 1997
[Fic] 75-30697

ISBN: 978-0-15-205822-7 hardcover
ISBN: 978-0-544-43958-0 paperback

Manufactured in the United States of America
DOC 10 9 8 7 6 5 4 3 2 1
4500527840

Contents

Illustrations

Also insets and tailpieces

Note

The Fifth of November is Guy Fawkes' Day in England. In peace-time it is celebrated with bonfires on the greens, fireworks in the parks and the carrying of "guys" through the streets. "Guys" are stuffed, straw figures of unpopular persons; and after they have been shown to everybody they are burnt in the bonfires amid great acclamation. The children black their faces and put on comical clothes, and go about begging for a Penny for the Guy. Only the very meanest people refuse to give pennies and these are always visited by Extreme Bad Luck.

The Original Guy Fawkes was one of the men who took part in the Gunpowder Plot. This was a conspiracy for blowing up King James I and the Houses of Parliament on November 5th, 1605. The plot was discovered, however, before any damage was done. The only result was that King James and his Parliament went on living but Guy Fawkes, poor man, did not. He was executed with the other conspirators. Nevertheless, it is Guy Fawkes who is re-membered today and King James who is forgotten. For since that time, the Fifth of November in England, like the Fourth of July in America, has been devoted to Fireworks. From 1605 till 1939 every village green in the shires had a bonfire on Guy Fawkes' Day. In the village where I live, in Sussex, we made our bonfire in the Vicarage paddock and every year, as soon as it was lit, the Vicar's cow would begin to dance. She danced while the flames roared up to the sky, she danced till the ashes were black and cold. And the next morning — it was always the same — the Vicar would have no milk for his breakfast. It is strange to think of a simple cow rejoicing so heartily at the saving of Parliament so many years ago.

Since 1939, however, there have been no bonfires on the village greens. No fireworks gleam in the blackened parks and the streets are dark and silent. But this darkness will not last forever. There will some day come a Fifth of November — or another date, it doesn't matter — when fires will burn in a chain of brightness from Land's End to John O'Groats. The children will dance and leap about them as they did in the times before. They will take each other by the hand and watch the rockets breaking, and afterwards they will go home singing to the houses full of light. . . .

P. L. T. (1943)

CHAPTER ONE

The Fifth of November*

I t was one of those bleak and chilly mornings that remind you winter is coming. Cherry-Tree Lane was quiet and still. The mist hung over the Park like a shadow. All the houses looked exactly alike as the grey fog wrapped them round. Admiral Boom's flagstaff, with the telescope at the top of it, had entirely disappeared.

The Milkman, as he turned into the Lane, could hardly see his way.

"Milk Be-l-o-o-ow!" he called, outside the Admiral's door. And his voice sounded so queer and hollow that it gave him quite a fright.

"I'll go 'ome till the fog lifts," he said to himself. " 'Ere! Look where you're goin'!" he went on, as a shape loomed suddenly out of the mist and bumped against his shoulder.

"Bumble, bumble, bum-bur-um-bumble," said a gentle, muffled voice.

"Oh, it's you!" said the Milkman, with a sigh of relief.

*See note on pages xiii–xiv

"Bumble," remarked the Sweep again. He was holding his brushes in front of his face to keep his moustache dry.

"Out early, aren't you?" the Milkman said.

The Sweep gave a jerk of his black thumb towards Miss Lark's house.

"Had to do the chimbley before the dogs had breakfast. In case the soot gave them a cough," he explained.

The Milkman laughed rudely. For that was what everybody did when Miss Lark's two dogs were mentioned.

The mist went wreathing through the air. There was not a sound in the Lane.

"Ugh!" said the Milkman, shivering. "This quiet gives me the 'Orrors!"

And as he said that, the Lane woke up. A sudden roar came from one of the houses and the sound of stamping feet.

"That's Number Seventeen!" said the Sweep. "Excuse me, old chap. I think I'm needed." He cautiously felt his way to the gate and went up the garden path. . . .

Inside the house, Mr. Banks was marching up and down, kicking the hall furniture.

"I've had about all I can stand!" he shouted, waving his arms wildly.

"You keep on saying that," Mrs. Banks cried. "But you won't tell me what's the matter." She looked at Mr. Banks anxiously.

"Everything's the matter!" he roared. "Look at this!" He waggled his right foot at her. "And this!" he went on, as he waggled his left.

Mrs. Banks peered closely at the feet. She was rather short-sighted and the hall was misty.

"I — er — don't see anything wrong," she began timidly.

"Of course you don't!" he said, sarcastically. "It's only imagination, of course, that makes me think Robertson Ay has given me one black shoe and one brown!" And again he waggled his feet.

"Oh!" said Mrs. Banks hurriedly. For now she saw clearly what the trouble was.

"You may well say 'Oh!' So will Robertson Ay when I give him the sack tonight."

"It's not his fault, Daddy!" cried Jane, from the stairs. "He couldn't see — because of the fog. Besides, he's not strong."

"He's strong enough to make my life a misery!" said Mr. Banks angrily.

"He needs rest, Daddy!" Michael reminded him, hurrying down after Jane.

"He'll get it!" promised Mr. Banks, as he snatched up his bag. "When I think of the things I could have done if I hadn't gone and got married! Lived alone in a Cave, perhaps. Or I might have gone Round the World."

"And what would *we* have done, then?" asked Michael.

"You would have had to fend for yourselves. And serve you right! Where's my overcoat?"

"You have it on, George," said Mrs. Banks, meekly.

"Yes!" he retorted. "And only one button! But anything's good enough for *me! I'm* only the man who Pays the Bills. I shall not be home for dinner."

A wail of protest went up from the children.

"But it's Guy Fawkes' Day," wheedled Mrs. Banks. "And you so good at letting off rockets."

"No rockets for me!" cried Mr. Banks. "Nothing but trouble from morning till night!" He shook Mrs. Banks' hand from his arm and dashed out of the house.

"Shake, sir!" said the Sweep in a friendly voice as Mr. Banks knocked into him, "It's lucky, you know, to shake hands with a Sweep."

"Away, away!" said Mr. Banks wildly. "This is not my lucky day!"

The Sweep looked after him for a moment. Then he smiled to himself and rang the door-bell. . . .

"He doesn't mean it, does he, Mother? He *will* come home for the fireworks!" Jane and Michael rushed at Mrs. Banks and tugged at her skirt.

"Oh, I can't promise anything, children!" she sighed, as she looked at her face in the front hall mirror.

And she thought to herself — Yes, I'm getting thinner. One of my dimples has gone already and soon I shall lose

the second. No one will look at me any more. And it's all
her fault!

By her, Mrs. Banks meant Mary Poppins, who had been
the children's nurse. As long as Mary Poppins was in the
house, everything had gone smoothly. But since that day
when she had left them — so suddenly and without a Word
of Warning — the family had gone from Bad to Worse.

Here am I, thought Mrs. Banks miserably, with five wild
children and no one to help me. I've advertised. I've asked
my friends. But nothing seems to happen. And George is
getting crosser and crosser; and Annabel's teething; and

Jane and Michael and the Twins are so naughty, not to mention that awful Income Tax——

She watched a tear run over the spot where the dimple had once been.

"It's no good," she said, with sudden decision. "I shall have to send for Miss Andrew."

A cry went up from all four children. Away in the Nursery, Annabel screamed. For Miss Andrew had once been their Father's governess and they knew how frightful she was.

"I won't speak to her!" shouted Jane, in a rage.

"I'll spit on her shoes if she comes!" threatened Michael.

"No, no!" wailed John and Barbara miserably.

Mrs. Banks clapped her hands to her ears. "Children, have mercy!" she cried in despair.

"Beg pardon, ma'am," said Ellen the housemaid, as she tapped Mrs. Banks on the shoulder. "The Sweep is 'ere for the Drawing-room Chimbley. But I warn you, ma'am, it's my Day Out! And I can't clean up after 'im. So there!" She blew her nose with a trumpeting sound.

"Excuse me!" said the Sweep cheerfully, as he dragged in his bags and brushes.

" 'Oo's that?" came the voice of Mrs. Brill as she hurried up from the kitchen. "The Sweep? On Baking Day? No, you don't! I'm sorry to give you notice, ma'am. But if that Hottentot goes into the chimney, I shall go out of the door."

Mrs. Banks glanced round desperately.

"I didn't ask him to come!" she declared. "I don't even know if the chimney wants sweeping!"

"A chimbley's always glad of a brush." The Sweep stepped calmly into the Drawing-room and began to spread out his sheet.

Mrs. Banks looked nervously at Mrs. Brill. "Perhaps Robertson Ay could help — " she began.

"Robertson is asleep in the pantry, wrapped in your best lace shawl. And nothing will wake him," said Mrs. Brill, "but the sound of the Last Trombone. So, if you please, I'll be packing my bag. 'Ow! Let me go, you Hindoo!"

For the Sweep had seized Mrs. Brill's hand and was shaking it vigorously. A reluctant smile spread over her face.

"Well — just this once!" she remarked cheerfully. And she went down the kitchen stairs.

The Sweep turned to Ellen with a grin.

"Don't touch me, you black heathen!" she screamed in a terrified voice. But he took her hand in a firm grip and she, too, began to smile. "Well, no messing up the carpet!" she warned him, and hurried off to her work.

"Shake!" said the Sweep, as he turned to the children. "It's sure to bring you luck!" He left a black mark on each of their palms and they all felt suddenly better.

Then he put out his hand to Mrs. Banks. And as she

took his warm black fingers her courage came flowing back.

"We must make the best of things, darlings," she said. "I shall advertise for another nurse. And perhaps something good will happen."

Jane and Michael sighed with relief. At least she was not going to send for Miss Andrew.

"What do you do when *you* need luck?" asked Jane, as she followed the Sweep to the Drawing-room.

"Oh, I just shake 'ands with meself," he said, cheerfully, pushing his brush up the chimney.

All day long the children watched him and argued over who should hand him the brushes. Now and again Mrs. Banks came in, to complain of the noise and hurry the Sweep.

And all day long, beyond the windows, the mist crept through the Lane. Every sound was muffled. The birds were gone. Except for an old and moulting Starling who kept on peering through the cracks in the blinds as if he were looking for someone.

At last the Sweep crept out of the chimney and smiled at his handiwork.

"So kind of you!" said Mrs. Banks hurriedly. "Now, I'm sure you must want to pack up and go home —— "

"*I'm* in no 'Urry," remarked the Sweep. "Me Tea isn't ready till six o'clock and I've got an hour to fill in —— "

"Well, you can't fill it in here!" Mrs. Banks shrieked.

"I have to tidy up this room before my husband comes home!"

"I tell you what —" the Sweep said calmly. "If you've got a rocket or two about you, I could take them children into the Park and show 'em a few fireworks. It'd give you a rest and meself a Treat. I've always been very partial to rockets, ever since a boy — and before!"

A yell of delight went up from the children. Michael ran to a window and lifted the blind.

"Oh, look what's happened!" he cried in triumph.

For a change had come to Cherry-Tree Lane. The chill grey mist had cleared away. The houses were lit with warm soft lights. And away in the West shone a glimmer of sunset, rosy and clear and bright.

"Remember your coats!" cried Mrs. Banks, as the children darted away. Then she ran to the cupboard under the staircase and brought out a nobbly parcel.

"Here you are!" she said breathlessly to the Sweep. "And, mind, be careful of sparks!"

"Sparks?" said the Sweep. "Why, sparks is my 'Obby. Them and the soot wot comes after!"

The children leapt like puppies about him as he went down the garden path. Mrs. Banks sat down for two minutes' rest on one of the sheet-covered chairs. The Starling looked in at her for a moment. Then he shook his head disappointedly and flew away again. . . .

Daylight was fading as they crossed the road. By the Park railings Bert, the Matchman, was spreading out his tray. He lit a candle with one of his matches and began to draw pictures on the pavement. He nodded gaily to the children as they hurried through the Gates.

"Now, all we need," the Sweep said fussily, "is a clear patch of grass —— "

"Which you won't get!" said a voice behind them. "The Park is closed at 5:30."

Out from the shadows came the Park Keeper, looking very belligerent.

"But it's Guy Fawkes' Day — the Fifth of November!" the children answered quickly.

"Orders is orders!" he retorted, "and all days are alike to me."

"Well, where can we let off the fireworks?" Michael demanded impatiently.

A greedy look leapt to the Keeper's eyes.

"You got some fireworks?" he said hungrily. "Well, why not say so before!" And he snatched the parcel from the Sweep and began to untie the string. "Matches — that's what we need!" he went on, panting with excitement.

"Here," said the Matchman's quiet voice. He had followed the children into the Park and was standing behind them with his lighted candle.

The Park Keeper opened a bundle of Squibs.

"They're *ours,* you know!" Michael reminded him.

"Ah, let me help you — do!" said the Keeper. "I've never 'ad fun on Guy Fawkes' Day — never since I was a boy!"

And without waiting for permission, he lit the Squibs at the Matchman's candle. The hissing streams of fire poured out, and pop, pop, pop, went the crackers. The Park Keeper seized a Catherine Wheel and stuck it on a branch. The rings of light began to turn and sparkled on the air. And after that he was so excited that nothing could stop him. He went on lighting fuse after fuse as though he had gone mad.

Flower Pots streamed from the dewy grass and Golden Rain flowed down through the darkness. Top Hats burned for a bright short moment; Balloons went floating up to the branches; and Firesnakes writhed in the shadows. The children jumped and squeaked and shouted. The Park Keeper ran about among them like a large frenzied dog. And amid the noise and the sparkling lights the Matchman waited quietly. The flame of his candle never wavered as they lit their fuses from it.

"Now!" cried the Keeper, who was hoarse with shouting. "Now we come to the rockets!"

All the other fireworks had gone. Nothing remained in the nobbly parcel except three long black sticks.

"No you don't!" said the Sweep, as the Keeper snatched them. "Share and share. That's fair!" He gave the Keeper one rocket and kept the others for himself and the children.

"Make way, make way!" said the Keeper importantly, as he lit the fuse at the candle flame and stuck the stick in the ground.

Hissing and guttering, the spark ran down like a little golden thread. Then — whoop! went the stick as it shot away. Up in the sky the children heard a small faraway bang. And a swirl of red-and-blue stars broke out and rained upon the Park.

"Oh!" cried the children. And "Oh!" cried the Sweep. For that is the only word anyone can say when a rocket's stars break out.

Then it was the Sweep's turn. The candle-light gleamed on his black face as he lit the fuse of his rocket. Then came a whoop and another bang and white-and-green stars spread over the sky like the ribs of a bright umbrella. And again the watchers all cried "Oh!" and sighed for sheer joy.

"It's our turn now!" cried Jane and Michael. And their fingers trembled as they lit the fuse. They pressed the stick down into the earth and stepped back to watch. The thread of golden fire ran down. Whe-e-e-ew! Up went the stick with a singing sound, up to the very top of the sky. And Jane and Michael held their breath as they waited for it to burst.

At last, far away and very faint, they heard the little bang.

Now for the stars, they thought to themselves.

But — alas! — nothing happened.

"Oh!" said everyone again — not for joy this time, but for disappointment. For no stars broke from the third rocket. There was nothing but darkness and the empty sky.

"Tricksy — that's what they are!" said the Sweep. "There are some as just doesn't go off! Well, come on home, all. There's no good staring. Nothing will come down now!"

"Closing Time! Everyone out of the Park!" cried the Park Keeper importantly.

But Jane and Michael took no notice. They stood there watching, hand in hand. For their hopeful eyes had noticed something that nobody else had seen. Up in the sky a tiny spark hovered and swayed in the darkness. What could it be? Not the stick of the rocket, for that must have fallen long ago. And certainly not a star, they thought, for the little spark was moving.

"Perhaps it's a special kind of rocket that has only one spark," said Michael.

"Perhaps," Jane answered quietly, as she watched the tiny light.

They stood together, gazing upwards. Even if there was only one spark they would watch till it went out. But, strangely enough, it did not go out. In fact, it was growing larger.

"Let's get a move on!" urged the Sweep. And again the Park Keeper cried:

"Closing Time!"

But still they waited. And still the spark grew ever larger and brighter. Then suddenly Jane caught her breath. And Michael gave a gasp. Oh, was it possible — ? Could it be — ? they silently asked each other.

Down came the spark, growing longer and wider. And as it came, it took on a shape that was strange and also familiar. Out of the glowing core of light emerged a curious figure — a figure in a black straw hat and a blue coat trimmed with silver buttons — a figure that carried in one hand something that looked like a carpet bag, and in the other — oh, could it be true? — a parrot-headed umbrella.

Behind them the Matchman gave a cry and ran through the Park Gates.

The curious figure was drifting now to the tops of the

naked trees. Its feet touched the highest bough of an oak and stepped down daintily through the branches. It stood for a moment on the lowest bough and balanced itself neatly.

Jane and Michael began to run and their breath broke from them in a happy shout.

"Mary Poppins! Mary Poppins! Mary Poppins!" Half-laughing, half-weeping, they flung themselves upon her.

"You've c-come b-back, at l-last!" stammered Michael excitedly, as he clutched her neatly shod foot. It was warm and bony and quite real and it smelt of Black Boot-polish.

"We knew you'd come back. We trusted you!" Jane seized Mary Poppins' other foot and dragged at her cotton stocking.

Mary Poppins' mouth crinkled with the ghost of a smile. Then she looked at the children fiercely.

"I'll thank you to let go my shoes!" she snapped. "I am not an object in a Bargain Basement!"

She shook them off and stepped down from the tree, as John and Barbara, mewing like kittens, rushed over the grass towards her.

"Hyenas!" she said with an angry glare, as she loosened their clutching fingers. "And what, may I ask, are you all doing — running about in the Park at night and looking like Blackamoors?"

Quickly they pulled out handkerchiefs and began to rub their cheeks.

"My fault, Miss Poppins," the Sweep apologised. "I been sweeping the Drawing-room chimbley."

"Somebody will be sweeping *you*, if you don't look out!" she retorted.

"But-but! Glog-glog! Er-rumph! Glug-glug!" Speechless with astonishment, the Park Keeper blocked their path.

"Out of my way, please!" said Mary Poppins, haughtily brushing him aside as she pushed the children in front of her.

"This is the Second Time!" he gasped, suddenly finding his voice. "First it's a Kite and now it's a — You can't do things like this, I tell you! It's against the Law. And, furthermore, it's all against Nature."

Out of the glowing core of light emerged a curious figure

He flung out his hand in a wild gesture and Mary Poppins popped into it a small piece of cardboard.

"Wot's this?" he demanded, turning it over.

"My Return Ticket," she calmly replied.

And Jane and Michael looked at each other and nodded wisely together.

"Ticket — wot ticket? Buses have tickets and so do trains. But you came down on I-don't-know-what! Where did you come from? 'Ow did you get 'ere? That's what I want to know!"

"Curiosity Killed a Cat!" said Mary Poppins primly. She pushed the Park Keeper to one side and left him staring at the little green ticket as though it were a ghost.

The children danced and leapt about her as they came to the Park Gates.

"Walk quietly, please," she told them crossly. "You are not a School of Porpoises! And which of you, I'd like to know, has been playing with lighted candles?"

The Matchman scrambled up from his knees.

"I lit it, Mary," he said eagerly. "I wanted to write you a —— " He waved his hands. And there on the pavement, not quite finished, was the one word

WELCOM

Mary Poppins smiled at the coloured letters. "That's a lovely greeting, Bert," she said softly.

The Matchman seized her black-gloved hand, and looked at her eagerly. "Shall I see you on Thursday, Mary?" he asked.

She nodded. "Thursday, Bert," she said. Then she flung a withering look at the children. "No dawdling, if you please!" she commanded, as she hurried them across the Lane to Number Seventeen.

Up in the Nursery Annabel was screaming her head off. Mrs. Banks was running along the hall, calling out soothing phrases. As the children opened the Front Door, she gave one look at Mary Poppins, and collapsed upon the stairs.

"Can it be you, Mary Poppins?" she gasped.

"It can, ma'am," Mary Poppins said calmly.

"But — where did you spring from?" Mrs. Banks cried.

"She sprang right out of a —— " Michael was just about to explain when he felt Mary Poppins' eyes upon him. He knew very well what that look meant. He stammered and was silent.

"I came from the Park, ma'am," said Mary Poppins, with the patient air of a martyr.

"Thank goodness!" breathed Mrs. Banks from her heart. Then she remembered all that had happened since Mary Poppins had left them. I mustn't seem *too* pleased, she thought. Or she'll be more uppish than ever!

"You left me Without a Word, Mary Poppins," she said with an air of dignity. "I think you might tell me when you're coming and going. I never know where I am."

"Nobody does, ma'am," said Mary Poppins, as she calmly unbuttoned her gloves.

"Don't *you*, Mary Poppins?" asked Mrs. Banks, in a very wistful voice.

"Oh, *she* knows," Michael answered daringly. Mary Poppins gave him an angry glare.

"Well, you're here now, anyway!" Mrs. Banks cried. She felt extremely relieved. For now she need neither advertise nor send for Miss Andrew.

"Yes, ma'am. Excuse me," said Mary Poppins.

And she neatly stepped past Mrs. Banks and put her carpet bag on the bannisters. It slid up swiftly with a whistling sound and bounced into the Nursery. Then she gave the umbrella a little toss. It spread its black silk wings like a bird and flew up after the carpet bag with a parrot-like squawk.

The children gave an astonished gasp and turned to see if their Mother had noticed.

But Mrs. Banks had no thought for anything but to get to the telephone.

"The Drawing-room chimney has been cleaned. We are having Lamb Chops and peas for dinner. And Mary Poppins is back!" she cried, breathlessly.

"I don't believe it!" crackled Mr. Banks' voice. "I shall come and see for myself!"

Mrs. Banks smiled happily as she hung up the receiver. . . .

Mary Poppins went primly up the stairs and the children tore past her into the Nursery. There on the hearth lay the carpet bag. And standing in its usual corner was the parrot-headed umbrella. They had a settled, satisfied air as though they had been there for years. In the cradle, Annabel, blue in the face, was tying herself into knots. She stared in surprise at Mary Poppins, and smiled a toothless smile. Then she put on her Innocent Angel look and began to play tunes on her toes.

"Humph!" said Mary Poppins grimly, as she put her straw hat in its paper bag. She took off her coat and hung it up on the hook behind the door. Then she glanced at herself in the Nursery mirror and stooped to unlock the carpet bag.

It was quite empty except for a curled-up Tape Measure.

"What's that for, Mary Poppins?" asked Jane.

"To measure you," she replied quickly. "To see how you've grown."

"You needn't bother," Michael informed her. "We've all grown two inches. Daddy measured us."

"Stand straight, please!" Mary Poppins said calmly, ignoring the remark. She measured him from his head to his feet and gave a loud sniff.

"I might have known it!" she said, snorting. "You've grown Worse and Worse."

Michael stared. "Tape Measures don't tell words, they tell inches," he said, protestingly.

"Since when?" she demanded haughtily, as she thrust it under his nose. There on the Tape were the tell-tale words in big blue letters:

W-O-R-S-E A-N-D W-O-R-S-E

"Oh!" he said, in a horrified whisper.

"Head up, please!" said Mary Poppins, stretching the Tape against Jane.

"Jane has grown into a Wilful, Lazy, Selfish child," she read out in triumph.

The tears came pricking into Jane's eyes. "Oh, I haven't, Mary Poppins!" she cried. For, funnily enough, she only remembered the times when she had been good.

Mary Poppins slipped the Tape round the Twins. "Quarrelsome" was their measurement. "Fretful and Spoilt," was Annabel's.

"I thought so!" Mary Poppins said, sniffing. "I've only got to turn my back for you to become a Menagerie!"

She drew the Tape round her own waist; and a satisfied smile spread over her face.

"Better Than Ever. Practically Perfect," her own measurement read.

"No more than I expected," she preened. And added, with a furious glare, "Now, spit-spot into the Bathroom!"

They hurried eagerly to obey her. For now that Mary Poppins was back, everything went with a swing. They undressed and bathed in the wink of an eye. Nobody dawdled over Supper, nobody left a crumb or a drop. They pushed in their chairs, folded their napkins and scrambled into bed.

Up and down the Nursery went Mary Poppins, tucking them all in. They could smell her old familiar smell, a mixture of toast and starchy aprons. They could feel her old familiar shape, solid and real beneath her clothes. They watched her in adoring silence, drinking her in.

Michael, as she passed his bed, peered over the edge and under it. There was nothing there except dust and slippers. Then he peeped under Jane's bed. Nothing there, either.

"But where are you going to sleep, Mary Poppins?" he enquired curiously.

As he spoke, she touched the door of the clothes cupboard. It burst open noisily and out of it, with a graceful sweep, came the old camp bed. It was made up, ready to be slept in. And upon it, in a neat pile, were Mary Poppins' possessions. There were the Sun-light Soap and the hair-pins, the bottle of scent, the folding armchair, the tooth-brush and the lozenges. The nightgowns, cotton, and flan-nel as well, were tidily laid on the pillow. And beside them were the boots and the dominoes, and the bathing-caps and the postcard album.

The children sat up in a gaping row.

"But how did it get in there?" demanded Michael. "There wasn't a sign of it today. I know, 'cos I hid there from Ellen!"

He dared not go on with his questions, however, for Mary Poppins looked so haughty that the words froze on his lips. With a sniff, she turned away from him and un-folded a flannel nightgown.

Jane and Michael looked at each other. And their eyes said all that their tongues could not: It's no good expecting her to explain, they told each other silently.

They watched her comical scarecrow movements as she undressed beneath the nightgown. Clip, clip — the buttons flew apart. Off went her petticoat — swish, swish, swish! A peaceful feeling stole into the children. And they knew that it came from Mary Poppins. Dreamily watch-ing the wriggling nightgown, they thought of all that had happened. How she had first arrived at the house, blown by the West Wind. How her umbrella had carried her off when the wind went round to the East. They thought how she had come back to them on the day when they flew the Kite; and how she had ridden away once more and left them lonely for her comforting presence.

Well, now — they sighed happily — she was back again, and just the same as ever. Here she was, settling down in the Nursery, as calmly as though she had never left it. The thoughts he was thinking rose up in Michael like bubbles in soda water. And before he could stop them, they burst right out.

"Oh, Mary Poppins," he cried, eagerly, "it's been just awful without you!"

Her lip quivered. It seemed as though a smile might break out. But it changed its mind and didn't.

"*You've* been awful — that's more like it! This house is nothing but a Bear Garden. I wonder anyone stays in it!"

"But *you* will, won't you?" he said wheedlingly.

"We'll be good as gold, if only you'll stay!" Jane promised solemnly.

She looked from one to the other calmly, seeing right down inside their hearts and understanding everything.

"I'll stay —— " she said, after a little pause. "I'll stay till the door opens." And as she spoke she gazed thoughtfully at the door of the Nursery.

Jane gave a little anxious cry. "Oh, don't say that, Mary Poppins!" she wailed. "That door is always opening!"

Mary Poppins glared.

"I meant the Other Door," she said, as she buttoned up her nightgown.

"What can she mean?" Jane whispered to Michael.

"I know what she means," he answered cleverly. "There isn't any other door. And a door that isn't there, *can't* open. So she's going to stay forever." He hugged himself happily at the thought.

Jane, however, was not so sure. I wonder, she thought to herself.

But Michael went on cheerfully babbling.

"I'm glad I shook hands with the Sweep," he said. "It brought us wonderful luck. Perhaps he'll do the Nursery next and shake hands with *you*, Mary Poppins!"

"Pooh!" she replied, with a toss of her head. "I don't need any luck, thank you!"

"No," he said thoughtfully, "I suppose you don't. Anyone who can come out of a rocket — as you did tonight — must be born lucky. I mean — er — oh, don't *look* at me!"

He gave a little beseeching cry, for Mary Poppins was glaring at him in a way that made him shudder. Standing there in her flannel nightgown, she seemed to freeze him in his cosy bed.

"I wonder if I heard you correctly?" she enquired in an icy voice. "Did I understand you to mention *Me* — in connection with a Rocket?" She said the word "Rocket" in such a way as to make it seem quite shocking.

In terror, Michael glanced about him. But no help came

from the other children. And he knew he would have to go through with it.

"But you did, Mary Poppins!" he protested bravely. "The rocket went pop! and there you were, coming out of it down the sky!"

She seemed to grow larger as she came towards him.

"Pop?" she repeated, furiously. "I popped — and came out of a rocket?"

He shrank back feebly against the pillow. "Well — that's what it looked like — didn't it, Jane?"

"Hush!" whispered Jane, with a shake of her head. She knew it was no good arguing.

"I have to say it, Mary Poppins! We saw you!" Michael wailed. "And if *you* didn't come out of the rocket, what did! There weren't any stars!"

"Pop!" said Mary Poppins again. "Out of a rocket with a pop! You have often insulted me, Michael Banks, but this is the Very Worst. If I hear any more about Pops — or Rockets —— " She did not tell him what she would do but he knew it would be dreadful.

"Wee-twee! Wee-twee!"

A small voice sounded from the window-sill. An old Starling peered into the Nursery and flapped his wings excitedly.

Mary Poppins bounded to the window.

"Be off, you sparrer!" she said fiercely. And as the Starling darted away she switched out the light and pounced into bed. They heard her angrily muttering "Pop!" as she pulled the blankets up.

Then silence settled over them like a soft comforting cloud. It had almost folded them to sleep when the faintest murmur came from Jane's bed.

"Michael!" she said, in a careful whisper.

He sat up cautiously and looked in the direction of her pointing finger.

From the corner by the fireplace came a little glow of light. And they saw that the folds of the parrot umbrella were full of coloured stars — the kind of stars you expect to see when a rocket breaks in the sky. Their eyes grew wide with astonishment as the parrot's head bent down. Then, one by one, its beak plucked the stars from the silken folds and threw them on the floor. They gleamed for a moment, gold and silver, then faded and went out. Then the parrot head straightened upon the handle, and Mary Poppins' black umbrella stood stiff and still in its corner.

The children looked at each other and smiled. But they said nothing. They could only wonder and be silent. They knew there were not enough words in the Dictionary for the things that happened to Mary Poppins.

"Tick-tock!" said the clock on the mantelpiece. "Go to sleep, children! Tick, tock, tick!"

Then they closed their eyes on the happy day and the clock kept time with their quiet breathing.

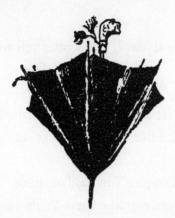

Mr. Banks sat and snored in his study with a newspaper over his face.

Mrs. Banks was sewing new black buttons on his old overcoat.

"Are you still thinking what you might have done if you hadn't got married?" she asked.

"Eh, what?" said Mr. Banks, waking up. "Well, no. It's much too much trouble. And now that Mary Poppins is back, I shan't have to think about anything."

"Good," said Mrs. Banks, sewing briskly. "And I'll try and teach Robertson Ay."

"Teach him what?" Mr. Banks said, sleepily.

"Not to give you one black and one brown, of course!"

"You'll do nothing of the kind," Mr. Banks insisted. "The mixture was much admired at the Office. I shall always wear them that way in future."

"Indeed?" said Mrs. Banks, smiling happily. On the whole, she felt glad Mr. Banks had married. And now that

Mary Poppins was back, she would tell him so more often. . . .

Downstairs in the kitchen sat Mrs. Brill. The Policeman had just brought Ellen home and was staying for a Cup of Tea.

"That Mary Poppins!" he said, sipping. "She's 'ere today and gone tomorrer, just like them Willy-the-Wisps!"

"Ow! Don't say that!" said Ellen, sniffling. "I thought she was come to stay."

The Policeman gave her his handkerchief.

"Maybe she will!" he told her fondly. "You never can tell, you know."

"Well, I'm sure I hope so," sighed Mrs. Brill. "This 'ouse is a Model Residence whenever she's in it."

"I hope so, too. I need a rest," said Robertson Ay to the brooms. And he snuggled down under Mrs. Banks' shawl and went to sleep again.

But what Mary Poppins hoped, none of them knew. For Mary Poppins, as everyone knows, never told anyone anything. . . .

CHAPTER TWO

Mr. Twigley's Wishes

h, do come on, Mary Poppins!" said Michael impatiently, as he danced up and down on the pavement.

Mary Poppins took no notice. She was standing in the Lane admiring her reflection in the brass plate on Dr. Simpson's gate.

"You look quite tidy!" Jane assured her.

"Tidy!" Mary Poppins snorted. Tidy in her new black hat with the blue bow? Tidy indeed! Handsome, she thought, would be nearer the mark. Tossing her head, she strode on quickly and they had to run to keep up with her.

The three of them were walking through the fine May afternoon to find Mr. Twigley. For the Drawing-room piano was out of tune and Mrs. Banks had asked Mary Poppins to find a piano-tuner.

"There's my cousin, Ma'am, Mr. Twigley. Just three blocks from here." Mary Poppins had announced. And when Mrs. Banks said she had never heard of him, Mary

Poppins, with her usual sniff, had reminded Mrs. Banks that *her* relatives were composed of the Very Best People.

And now Jane and Michael, who had already met two members of Mary Poppins' family, were wondering what Mr. Twigley would be like.

"I think he will be tall and thin, like Mr. Turvy," said Michael.

"I think he will be round and fat, like Mr. Wigg," said Jane.

"I never knew such a pair for thinking!" said Mary Poppins. "You'll wear your brains out. Turn here, please!"

They hurried along and turned a corner and found themselves standing in a narrow street lined with small, old-fashioned houses.

"Why, what street is this? I never saw it before! And I've been here lots of times!" cried Jane.

"Well, don't blame *me*!" Mary Poppins snapped. "You don't suppose I put it there!"

"I shouldn't wonder if you did!" said Michael, as he gazed at the strange little houses. Then he added, with a flattering smile, "You're so very clever, you know!"

"Humph!" she said tartly, though her mouth took on a conceited look. "Clever is as clever does. And it's more than you are, anyway!" And, sniffing, she led them down the street and rang the bell of one of the houses.

"Pang!" said the bell loudly. And at the same moment

an upstairs window swung open. A large head, with a knob of hair at the back, popped out like a Jack-in-the-Box.

"Well, what's the matter now?" a harsh voice cried. Then the woman looked down and spied Mary Poppins. "Oh, it's you, is it?" she said angrily. "Well, you can just turn round and go back to wherever you came from. He isn't in!" The window swung to and the head disappeared.

The children felt very disappointed.

"Perhaps we can come again tomorrow," said Jane anxiously.

"Today — or Never. That's my motto!" snapped Mary Poppins. And she rang the bell again.

This time it was the front door that burst open. The owner of the head stood before them glowering. She wore large black boots, a blue-and-white checked apron and a black shawl round her shoulders. Jane and Michael thought she was the ugliest person they had ever seen. And they felt very sorry for Mr. Twigley.

"What — you again!" the huge woman shouted. "I told you he wasn't in. And in he is not, or my name's not Sarah Clump!"

"Then you aren't Mrs. Twigley!" exclaimed Michael, with relief.

"Not *yet*," she remarked, with an ominous smile. "Here! Down you come, all of you!" she added. For Mary Poppins, with the speed of a serpent, had slipped through the doorway and was dragging the children up the stairs. "Do you hear me? I'll have the Law on you, bursting into a decent woman's house like a set of Vampires!"

"Decent!" said Mary Poppins, snorting. "If you're decent I'm a Dromedary!" And she rapped three times on a door at her right.

"Who's there?" called an anxious voice from within. Jane and Michael trembled with excitement. Perhaps Mr. Twigley was at home, after all!

"It's me, Cousin Fred. Unlock the door, please!"

There was a moment's silence. Then the sound of a key being turned in the lock. The door opened and Mary Poppins, pulling the children after her, shut it and locked it again.

"Let me in — you Pirate!" roared Mrs. Clump, angrily rattling the handle.

Mary Poppins laughed quietly. The children glanced about them. They were in a large attic littered with scraps of wood, tins of paint and bottles of glue. Every available space in the room was filled with musical instruments. A harp stood in one corner and in another was a pile of drums. Trumpets and violins hung from the rafters; flutes and tin-whistles were stacked on the shelves. A dusty table by the window was littered with carpenter's tools. And on

the edge of the bench was a small polished box with a tiny screw-driver tossed beside it.

In the middle of the floor stood five half-finished musical boxes. Brightly they shone in their fresh new colours and round them, chalked on the boards in large white letters, were the words

WET PAINT

The whole attic smelt deliciously of wood-shavings, paint and glue. There was only one thing missing from it. And that was Mr. Twigley.

"Will you let me in or shall I go for the Police?" shouted Mrs. Clump, banging again. Mary Poppins took no notice. And presently they heard her thumping downstairs, muttering furiously as she went.

"Has she gone?" a thin voice cackled anxiously.

"She's gone downstairs and I've locked the door! Now, what have you done with yourself, please, Fred?" Mary Poppins gave an impatient sniff.

"I've wished, Mary!" chirped the voice again.

Jane and Michael stared round the dusty attic. Where *could* Mr. Twigley be?

"Oh, Fred! Don't tell me it's the —— ! Well, wish again, please, wherever you are! I haven't all day to waste."

"All right! I'm coming! No need for excitement!"

The violins played a stave of music. Then, out of the air — as it seemed to the children — came two short legs clad in baggy trousers. They were followed by a body in an old frock-coat. And last of all came a long white beard, a wrinkled face with glasses on its nose and a bald head in a smoking cap.

"Really, Cousin Fred!" said Mary Poppins crossly. "You're old enough to know better!"

"Nonsense, Mary!" said Mr. Twigley, beaming. "Nobody's ever old enough to know better! I'm sure you agree with me, young man!" He looked at Michael with his twinkly eyes. And Michael couldn't help twinkling back.

"But where were you hiding?" he demanded. "You couldn't have just come out of the air."

"Oh, yes, I could!" said Mr. Twigley. "If I wished," he added, as he skipped round the room.

"You mean, you just wished — and you disappeared?"

With a glance at the door, Mr. Twigley nodded.

"I had to — to get away from *her!*"

"Why? What would she do to you?" asked Jane.

"Why? Because she wants to marry me! She wants to get my wishes."

"Do you get everything you wish for?" asked Michael enviously.

"Oh, everything. That is, if I wish on the first New Moon, after the Second Wet Sunday, after the Third of May. And she —— " Mr. Twigley waved at the door. "*She*

wants me to wish for a Golden Palace and Peacock Pie every day for dinner. What would *I* do with a golden palace?
All that I want is —— "

"Be careful, Fred!" warned Mary Poppins.

Mr. Twigley clapped his hand to his mouth. "Tut, tut! I
really must remember! I've used up two wishes already!"

"How many do you get?" asked Jane.

"Seven," said Mr. Twigley, sighing. "My Godmother
thought that a suitable number. I know the old lady meant
it kindly. But I'd rather have had a Silver Mug. More useful.
And much less trouble."

"I'd rather have wishes," said Michael, stoutly.

"Oh, no, you wouldn't!" cried Mr. Twigley. "They're
tricky. And hard to handle. You think out the loveliest
things to ask for — then Supper Time comes and you're
feeling hungry and you find yourself wishing for Sausage
and Mashed!"

"What about the two you've already had? Were they any
good?" demanded Michael.

"Well, not so bad, now I come to think of it. I was working on my Birdie there —— " Mr. Twigley nodded towards his bench —— " when I heard *her* coming up the
stairs. 'Oh, Goodness!' I thought, 'I wish I could vanish!'
And — when I looked round, I wasn't there! It gave me
quite a turn for a moment. No wonder she told you I was
out!"

Mr. Twigley gave a happy cackle as he beamed at the

children and swung his coat-tails. They had never seen such a twinkly person. He seemed to them more like a star than a man.

"Then, of course," Mr. Twigley went on blandly, "I had to wish myself back again in order to see Mary Poppins! Now, Mary, what can I do for you?"

"Mrs. Banks would like her piano tuned, please, Fred. Number Seventeen, Cherry-Tree Lane, Opposite the Park," Mary Poppins said primly.

"Ah! Mrs. Banks. Then these must be——?" Mr. Twigley waved his hand at the children.

"They're Jane and Michael Banks," she explained, glancing at them with a look of disgust.

"Delighted. I call this a very great honour!" Mr. Twigley bowed and flung out his hands. "I wish I could offer you something to eat but I'm all at sixes and sevens today."

A flute rang gaily through the attic.

"What's this?" Mr. Twigley staggered back. In each of his upturned, outstretched hands lay a dish of Peaches-and-Cream.

Mr. Twigley stared. Then he sniffed at the peaches.

"There goes my third wish!" he said ruefully, as he handed the dishes to the children. "Well, it can't be helped. I've still got four more. And now I shall have to be really careful!"

"If you must waste wishes, Cousin Fred, I wish you would waste them on Bread and Butter. You'll spoil their Supper!" snapped Mary Poppins.

Jane and Michael spooned up their peaches hurriedly. They were not going to give Mr. Twigley the chance of wishing them away again.

"And now," said Mary Poppins, as the last mouthful disappeared. "Say Thank You to Mr. Twigley and we'll get along home."

"Oh, *no*, Mary! Why, you've only just come!" Mr. Twigley was so shocked that for once he stood quite still.

"Oh, do stay a little longer, Mary Poppins!" Jane and Michael begged. The thought of leaving Mr. Twigley all alone with his wishes was too much for them.

Mr. Twigley took Mary Poppins' hand.

"I feel so much safer when you're here, Mary! And it's ages since we've seen each other! Why not stay for a while — I wish you would!"

Jug, jug, jug, jug!

A shower of bird notes broke on the air. At the same moment the determined look on Mary Poppins' face changed to a polite smile. She took off her hat and laid it on the bench beside the glue-pot.

"Oh, my!" Mr. Twigley gasped in horror. "I've been and gone and done it again!"

"That's four!" cried Jane and Michael gaily, shouting with laughter at his look of surprise.

Four, four, four, four! The bird notes echoed.

"Dear me! How careless! I'm ashamed of myself!" For a moment Mr. Twigley looked almost sad. Then his face and his feet began to twinkle. "Well, it's no good crying over spilt wishes. We must just take care of the ones that are left. I'm coming, my Duckling! I'm coming, my Chick!" he called in the direction of the bird notes.

And, tripping to the dusty table, he took up the little polished box. His fingers touched a hidden spring. The lid flew open and the smallest, brightest bird the children had ever seen leapt up from a nest of gold. Clear jets of music poured from its beak. Its small throat throbbed with the stream of notes.

Jug, jug, jug, jug — tereu! it sang. And when the burning song was ended the bird dropped back to its golden nest.

"Oh, Mr. Twigley, what bird is that?" Jane looked at the box with shining eyes.

"A Nightingale," Mr. Twigley told her. "I was working on him when you came in. He has to be finished tonight, you see. Such lovely weather for nightingales."

"Why don't you just wish?" suggested Michael. "Then you needn't do any work."

"What! Wish on my Birdie? Certainly not! You see what happens when *I* start wishing. Why — he might turn into a Bald-headed Eagle!"

"Will you keep him to sing to you always?" Jane asked enviously. She wished she could have a bird like that.

"Keep him? Oh, dear, no! I'll set him free! Can't litter the place up with finished work. I've more things to do than take care of a bird. I have to put figures on those —— " he nodded at the half-finished musical boxes. "And I've got a rush order that *must* be finished — a music box playing 'A Day in the Park.'"

"A Day in the Park?" The children stared.

"The Band, you know!" Mr. Twigley explained. "And the sound of the fountains. And gossiping ladies. Rooks caw-cawing, and children laughing, and the slow, soft murmur of trees as they grow."

Mr. Twigley's eyes glowed behind his spectacles as he thought of all the lovely things he would put in the musical box.

"But you can't hear trees growing," protested Michael. "There's no music for that!"

"Tut!" said Mr. Twigley impatiently. "Of course there is! There's a music for everything. Didn't you ever hear the earth spinning? It makes a sound like a humming-top. Buckingham Palace plays 'Rule Britannia'; the River Thames is a drowsy flute. Dear me, yes! Everything in the world — trees, rocks and stars and human beings — they all have their own true music."

As he spoke Mr. Twigley tripped across the floor and wound up a musical box. Immediately the little platform at the top began to turn. And from within came a clear high piping like the sound of a penny whistle.

"That's mine!" said Mr. Twigley proudly, as he cocked his head to listen. He wound up another musical box and a new tune fell on the air.

"That's 'London Bridge Is Falling Down'! It's my favourite song!" cried Michael.

"What did I tell you?" smiled Mr. Twigley, as he turned another handle. The tune broke gaily from the box.

"That's mine!" said Jane, with a crow of delight. "It's 'Oranges and Lemons.'"

"Of course it is!" twinkled Mr. Twigley.

And gaily seizing the children's hands he swept them away across the attic. The three little platforms turned and spun and the three tunes mingled in the air.

> "London Bridge is Falling Down,
>   Dance over, my Lady Leigh!"

sang Michael.

> "Oranges and Lemons,
>   Said the Bells of St. Clements."

sang Jane.

And Mr. Twigley whistled like a happy blackbird.

The feet of the children were light as wings as they danced to their own true music. Never before, they told themselves, had they felt so light and merry.

Bang! The front door slammed and shook the house. Mr. Twigley paused on one toe and listened. Thump!

Thump! came the footsteps on the stairs. A loud voice rumbled across the landing.

Mr. Twigley gave a gasp of horror, and swung his coat-tails over his ears.

"She's coming!" he shrieked. "Oh, dear! Oh, my! I wish I were in a nice safe place!"

A blast of music came from the trumpets. And then a strange thing happened.

Mr. Twigley, as though by an unseen hand, was snatched from the floor of the attic. Off he went, hurtling past the children, like a seed of thistledown tossed by the wind. Then choking and gasping, shaking and panting, he landed upon his musical box. He did not seem to have grown smaller nor the box larger. Yet, somehow, they fitted perfectly together.

Round and round Mr. Twigley spun and upon his face spread a smile of triumph.

"I'm safe!" he yelled, as he waved to the children, "She'll never catch me now!"

"Hooray!" they were just about to shout but the word was caught in their throats, like a hiccup. For something had seized them by the hair and was flinging them both across the attic. Their arms and legs went sprawling wildly as they landed upon their musical boxes. They wobbled a little for a moment, but soon they were steadily whirling round.

"Oh!" panted Jane. "What a lovely surprise!"

"I feel like a spinning top!" shouted Michael.

Mr. Twigley gave a little start and stared at them in astonishment.

"Did *I* do that? Good Gracious me! I'm getting quite clever at wishing."

"Clever!" said Mary Poppins sniffing. "Ridiculous — that's what *I* call it!"

"Well, at least it's safe," said Mr. Twigley. "And rather pleasant. Why don't you try it?"

"Wish!" urged Michael, with a wave of his hand.

"Ah! *She* doesn't need to," said Mr. Twigley, with a curious glance at Mary Poppins.

"Well, if you insist . . ." she said with a sniff. And placing her two feet neatly together she rose from the floor and swept past the rafters. Then, without a smile, not even a wobble, she alighted upon a musical box. Immediately, though no one had wound it, the tune broke gaily out.

"Round and round the Cobbler's bench,
     The Monkey chased the Weasel,
  The Monkey said it was all in fun —
        Pop goes the Weasel!"

it sang.

And round and round went Mary Poppins, as calmly as though she had turned and spun from the very day she was born.

"Now we're all together!" Jane cried happily. She glanced

at the window and waved her hand to draw Michael's attention.

Outside in the street the little houses were revolving on their foundations. Above in the sky spun two white clouds. And the attic itself, like the musical boxes, was turning round and round.

But loudly though the four tunes rang, another sound could be heard above them. Thump! Thump! The heavy steps came nearer.

And the next moment somebody banged on the door.

"Open, I say, in the name of the Law!" cried a voice that was somehow familiar.

A strong hand twisted the rickety lock. And then, with a crash, the door burst open. On the threshold stood Mrs. Clump and the Policeman. They stared. Their eyes popped. Their mouths fell open with astonishment.

"Well, of all the shameful sights!" cried Mrs. Clump. "I never thought to see this house turned into an Amusement Park!" She shook her fist at Mary Poppins. "You're going to get your reward, my girl. The Policeman here will deal with you! And as for you, Mr. Twigley, down you get from that silly razzle-dazzle and comb your hair and put on your hat. We're going off to be married!"

Mr. Twigley shuddered. But he swung his coattails jauntily.

"Don't shout and thump

She alighted upon a musical box

Please, Mrs. Clump,
It makes me jump!"

he sang, as he sped round. The Policeman took out note-book and pencil.

"Come on! Stop spinning, all of you. I'm as giddy as a Garden Goat. And I want an Explanation!"

Mr. Twigley gave a gleeful cackle.

"You've come to the wrong place, Officer dear! I've nev-er yet made an Explanation. And what's more, as I used to say to my boy, Methuselah, I don't believe in 'em!"

"Now, now, joking'll only make things worse. You can't tell *me* you're Methuselah's father!" The Policeman smiled a knowing smile.

"Grandfather!" Mr. Twigley retorted, as he sailed grace-fully round.

"Now, that's enough. You just come down! This spin-ning and twirling is bad for the 'Ealth. And not permitted in Private Dwellings. 'Ere! 'Oo's that pulling me! Let me go!" The Policeman gave a frightened shriek as he shot off his feet and through the air. A music box broke into noisy song as he dropped like a stone upon it.

"Daisy, Daisy, give me your answer, do!
I've gone crazy, all for the love of you!"

it shouted.

" 'Elp! 'Elp! It's me — P.C. 32 calling!" The Policeman wildly snatched at his whistle and blew a resounding blast.

"Officer!" shouted Mrs. Clump. "You do your duty or I'll have the Law on you, too. Get down and arrest that woman!" She thrust a huge finger at Mary Poppins. "I'll have you put behind bars, my girl. I'll have you —— Here! Stop spinning me round!" Her eyes grew wide with angry amazement. For a curious thing was happening.

Slowly, on the spot where she stood, Mrs. Clump began to revolve. She had no musical box, no platform, she simply went round and round on the floor. The boards gave a loud protesting creak as the huge shape turned upon them.

"Well, that's fixed *you!*" cried Mr. Twigley.

> "Try and jump
> Dear Mrs. Clump!"

he advised her, with a gleeful shriek.

A shudder of horror shook Mrs. Clump as she tried to move her large black boots. She struggled. She writhed. She wriggled her body. But her feet were firmly glued to the floor.

"Clever girl, Mary! I'd never have thought of it!" Mr. Twigley smiled at Mary Poppins with pride and admiration.

"This is your doing — you wilful, wicked, cold-hearted Varmint!" Mrs. Clump gave an angry shout as she tried to clutch at Mary Poppins. "But I'll get even with you yet — or my name's not Sarah Clump!"

"It'll never be Twigley, anyway!" shrieked Mr. Twigley joyously.

"I want to go home! I want the Police Station!" wailed the Policeman, spinning madly.

"Well, nobody's keeping *you*, I'm sure!" said Mary Poppins, sniffing. As she spoke the Policeman's box came to a standstill and he stumbled off it, panting.

"Scotland Yard!" he cried, staggering to the door. "I must see the Chief! I must make a Report." And, blowing a frantic peal on his whistle, he fled downstairs and out of the house.

"Come back, you Villain!" screamed Mrs. Clump. "He's gone!" she went on, as the front door banged. "Oh, what shall I do? Help! Murder! Fire!"

Her face grew red as she tried to free herself. But it was no good. Her feet were firmly fixed to the floor, and she flung out her arms with a cry of anguish.

"Mr. Twigley!" she begged. "Please help me, Sir! I've always cooked you tasty meals. I've always kept you clean and tidy. You won't have to marry me, I promise. If you'll only wish something to set me free!"

"Be careful, Fred!" warned Mary Poppins, as she twirled in a dignified manner.

"A Wish in Time saves Nine! Now, let me think!" murmured Mr. Twigley.

He pressed his fingers to his eyes. Jane and Michael could see he was making an effort to wish Something Really Useful. For a moment he spun round, deep in thought. Then he looked up, smiling, and clapped his hands.

"Mrs. Clump," he cried gaily. "You *shall* be free! I wish for you a Golden Palace and Peacock Pie every day for dinner. But —— " he winked across at Mary Poppins, "my kind of palace, Mrs. Clump! And *my* kind of pie!"

A roll of drums boomed through the attic.

Mrs. Clump looked at Mary Poppins and smiled a smile of triumph.

"Aha!" she said smugly. "What did I tell you?"

But even as she spoke the proud smile faded. It changed to a look of purest terror.

For Mrs. Clump was no longer a large fat woman. Her buxom body was rapidly shrinking. Her feet as they spun on the creaking floor grew smaller with every turn.

"What's this?" she panted. "Oh, what can it be?" Her arms and her legs grew short and skinny as her figure dwindled to half its size.

"Police! Fire! Murder! S.O.S." Her voice grew thinner as she shrank.

"Oh, Mr. Twigley! What have you done? Police! Police!" squeaked the tiny voice.

As she spoke the floor gave an angry heave and flung her, spinning, into the air. She bounced back with a frantic shriek and stumbled away across the room. And as she ran she grew smaller than ever and her movements more and more jerky. One moment she was the size of a kitten and the next no bigger than a small-sized mouse. Away she went, stumbling and bouncing and tripping, till at the end of the attic she dashed into a tiny golden palace that had suddenly appeared.

"Oh, why did I speak to him? What has he done?" Mrs. Clump cried out in a tinny voice.

And looking through one of the golden windows, the children saw her collapse on a chair before a small tin pie. She began to cut it with jerky movements as the palace door closed with a bang.

At that moment the boxes ceased to spin. The music stopped and the attic was silent.

Down from his box sprang Mr. Twigley and ran to the golden palace. With a cry of delight he picked it up and gazed at the scene within.

"Very clever! I really must congratulate myself. All it needs now is a penny-in-the-slot and then it will do for Brighton Pier. One Penny, Only One Penny, folks! To see the Fat Woman Eating the Pie! Roll up! Roll up! Only one Penny!"

Waving the palace, Mr. Twigley went gaily capering round the room. Jane and Michael, leaping down from their boxes, ran after him and caught his coattails. They peered through the windows at Mrs. Clump. There was a look of horror on her mechanical face as she cut her mechanical pie.

"That was your sixth wish!" Michael reminded him.

"It was indeed!" Mr. Twigley agreed. "A Really useful idea, for once! Where there's a wish, there's a way, you see! Especially if *she's* around!" He nodded at Mary Poppins, who was stepping off her musical box in the most majestic manner.

"Get your hats, please!" she commanded sharply. "I want to get home for a Cup of Tea. I am not a Desert Camel."

"Oh, just one moment, please, Mary Poppins! Mr. Twigley's got one more wish!"

Jane and Michael, both talking at once, were tugging at her hands.

"Why, so I have! I'd quite forgotten. Now, what shall I —— ?"

"Cherry-Tree Lane, remember, Fred!" Mary Poppins' voice had a warning note.

"Oh, I'm glad you reminded me. Just a second!" Mr. Twigley put his hand to his brow and a scale of music sounded.

"What did you wish?" asked Jane and Michael.

But Mr. Twigley seemed suddenly to have become deaf, for he took no notice of the question. He shook hands hurriedly as though, having wished all his wishes, he was now anxious to be alone.

"You have to be going, you said? How sad! Is this your hat? Well, delighted you came! I hope — are these your gloves, dear Mary? — I hope you'll pay me another visit when my wishes come round again!"

"When will that be?" demanded Michael.

"Oh, in about ninety years or so." Mr. Twigley answered airily.

"But we'll be quite old by then!" said Jane.

"Maybe," he replied, with a little shrug. "But at least not as old as I am!"

And with that he kissed Mary Poppins on both cheeks and hustled them out of the room.

The last thing they saw was his jubilant smile as he

began to fix a Penny-in-the-Slot to Mrs. Clump's palace. . . .

Later, when they came to think about it, Jane and Michael could never remember how they got out of Mr. Twigley's house and into Cherry-Tree Lane. It seemed as though at one moment they were on the dusty stairs and the next were following Mary Poppins through the pearly evening light.

Jane glanced back for one last look at the little house.

"Michael!" she said in a startled whisper. "It's gone. Everything's gone!"

He looked round. Yes! Jane was right. The little street and the old-fashioned houses were nowhere to be seen. There was only the shadowy Park before them and the well-known curve of Cherry-Tree Lane.

"Well, where have we been all the afternoon?" said Michael, staring about him.

But it needed someone wiser than Jane to answer that question truly.

"We must have been somewhere," she said sensibly.

But that was not enough for Michael. He rushed away to Mary Poppins and pulled at her best blue skirt.

"Mary Poppins, where have we been today? What's happened to Mr. Twigley?"

"How should I know?" snapped Mary Poppins. "I'm not an Encyclopaedia."

"But he's gone! And the street's gone! And I suppose the musical box has gone, too — the one he went round on this afternoon!"

Mary Poppins stood still on the kerb, and stared.

"A cousin of mine on a musical box? What nonsense you do talk, Michael Banks!"

"But he did!" cried Jane and Michael together. "We *all* went round on musical boxes. Each of us to our own true music. And yours was 'Pop Goes the Weasel.' "

Her eyes blazed sternly through the darkness. She seemed to grow larger as she glared.

"Each to our — weasel? Round and round?" Really, she was so angry she could hardly get the words out.

"On top of a musical box, did you say? So, *this* is what I get for my pains! You spend the afternoon with a well-brought up, self-respecting pair like my cousin and myself. And all you can do afterwards is to make a mock of us. Round and round with a weasel, indeed! For Two Pins I'd leave you — here, on this spot — and never come back! I warn you!"

"On top of a musical weasel!" she fumed, as she stalked through the gathering dusk.

Snap, snap, went her heels along the pavement. Even her back had an angry look.

Jane and Michael hurried after her. It was no good arguing with Mary Poppins, especially when she looked like that. The best thing to do was to say nothing. And be glad there was nobody in the Lane to offer her Two Pins. In silence they walked along beside her, and thought of the afternoon's adventure and looked at each other and wondered. . . .

"Oh, Mary Poppins!" said Mrs. Banks brightly, as she opened the front door. "I'm sorry, but I don't need your cousin, after all. I tried the piano again just now. And it's quite in tune. In fact, better than ever."

"I'm glad of that, ma'am," said Mary Poppins, stealing a glance at herself in the mirror. "My cousin will make no charge."

"Well, I should think not!" cried Mrs. Banks indignantly. "Why, he hasn't even been here."

"Exactly, ma'am," said Mary Poppins. She sniffed as she turned towards the stairs.

Jane and Michael exchanged a secret look.

"That must have been the seventh wish!" Michael whispered. And Jane gave an answering nod.

Jug, jug, jug, jug — tereu!

From the Park came a shower of wild sweet music. It had a familiar sound.

"What can that be?" cried Mrs. Banks as she ran to the door to listen. "Good gracious! It's a Nightingale!"

Down from the branches fell the song, note by note, like plums from a tree. It burnt upon the evening air. It throbbed through the listening dusk.

"How very strange!" said Mrs. Banks. "They never sing in the city!"

Behind her back the children nodded and looked at each other wisely.

"It's Mr. Twigley's," murmured Jane.

"He's set it free!" answered Michael softly.

And they knew, as they listened to the burning song, that somewhere, somehow, Mr. Twigley was true — as true as his little golden bird that was singing now in the Park.

The Nightingale sang once more and was silent.

Mrs. Banks sighed and shut the door. "I wish I knew where he came from!" she said dreamily.

But Jane and Michael, who could have told her, were already half-way up the stairs. So they said nothing. There were things that could be explained, they knew, and things that could not be explained.

Besides, there were Currant Buns for Tea and they knew what Mary Poppins would say if they dared to keep her waiting. . . .

CHAPTER THREE

The Cat that Looked at a King

 ichael had toothache. He lay in bed groaning and looking at Mary Poppins out of the corner of his eye.

There she sat, in the old arm chair, busily winding wool. Jane knelt before her, holding the skein. Up from the garden came the cries of the Twins as they played on the lawn with Ellen and Annabel. It was quiet and peaceful in the Nursery. The clock made a clucking, satisfied sound like a hen that has laid an egg.

"Why should *I* have toothache and not Jane?" complained Michael. He pulled the scarf Mary Poppins had lent him more tightly round his cheek.

"Because you ate too many sweets yesterday," Mary Poppins replied tartly.

"But it was my Birthday!" he protested.

"A Birthday's no reason for turning yourself into a Dustbin! *I* don't have toothache after mine."

Michael glared at her. Sometimes he wished Mary

Poppins was not quite so Perfectly Perfect. But he never dared to say so.

"If I die," he warned her, "you'll be sorry. You'll wish you'd been a bit nicer!"

She sniffed contemptuously and went on winding.

Holding his cheek in his two hands he gazed round the Nursery. Everything there had the familiar look of an old friend. The wall paper, the rocking-horse, the worn red carpet. His eyes wandered to the mantelpiece.

There lay the Compass and the Doulton Bowl, the jam-jar full of daisies, the stick of his old Kite and Mary Poppins' Tape Measure. And there, too, was the present Aunt Flossie had given him yesterday — the little Cat of white china patterned with blue-and-green flowers. It sat there with its paws together and its tail neatly curled about them. The sunlight shone on its china back; its green eyes gazed gravely across the room. Michael gave it a friendly smile. He was fond of Aunt Flossie and he liked the present she had brought him.

Then his tooth gave another dreadful stab.

"Ow!" he shrieked, "It's digging a hole right into my gum!" He glanced pathetically at Mary Poppins. "And nobody cares!" he added bitterly.

Mary Poppins tossed him a mocking smile.

"Don't look at me like that!" he complained.

"Why not? A Cat can look at a King, I suppose!"

"But I'm not a king——" he grumbled crossly, "and

you're not a cat, Mary Poppins!" He hoped she would argue with him about it and take his mind off his tooth.

"Do you mean *any* cat can look at the King? Could Michael's cat?" demanded Jane.

Mary Poppins glanced up. Her blue eyes gazed at the Cat's green eyes and the Cat returned her look.

There was a pause.

"Any cat," said Mary Poppins at last. "But that cat more than most."

Smiling to herself, she took up the ball of wool again and something stirred on the mantelpiece. The china cat twitched its china whisker and lifted its head and yawned. The children could see its glistening teeth and a long pink cat's tongue. The Cat then arched its flowery back and stretched itself lazily. And after that, with a wave of its tail, it leapt from the mantelpiece.

Plop! went the four paws on the carpet. Purr! said the Cat as it crossed the hearth-rug. It paused for a moment by Mary Poppins and gave her a little nod. Then it sprang upon the window-sill, dived out into the shining sunlight and disappeared.

Michael forgot his toothache and gaped.

Jane dropped her skein and stared.

"But——" they both stammered. "How? Why? Where?"

"To see the Queen," Mary Poppins answered. "She's At Home every Second Friday. Don't stare like that,

Jane—the wind might change! Close your mouth, Michael! Your tooth will get cold."

"But I want to know what happened!" he cried. "He's made of china. He isn't real. And yet—he jumped! I saw him."

"Why did he want to see the Queen?" asked Jane.

"Mice," replied Mary Poppins calmly. "And partly for Old Sake's Sake."

A faraway look came into her eyes and the hands on the ball of wool fell idle. Jane flung a warning glance at Michael. He wriggled cautiously out of bed and crept across

the room. Mary Poppins took no notice. She was gazing
thoughtfully out of the window with distant dreamy eyes.

"Once upon a time," she began slowly, as though she
were reading from the sheet of sunlight. . . .

Once upon a time, there lived a King who thought he knew
practically everything. I couldn't even begin to tell you the
things he thought he knew. His head was as full of facts
and figures as a pomegranate of pips. And this had the ef-
fect of making the King extremely absent-minded. You
will hardly believe me when I say that he even forgot his
own name, which was Cole. The Prime Minister, however, had an excellent memory, and reminded him of it from
time to time.

Now, this King's favourite pursuit was thinking. He
thought all night and he thought in the morning. He
thought at mealtimes, he thought in his bath. He never noticed what was happening in front of his nose because, of
course, he was always thinking about something else.

And the things he thought about were not, as you might
imagine, the welfare of his people and how to make them
happy. Not at all. His mind was busy with other questions.
The number of baboons in India, for instance; and whether
the North Pole was as long as the South; and if pigs could
be taught to sing.

He not only worried about these things himself. He
forced everybody else to worry about them, too. All except

the Prime Minister, who was not at all a thinking kind of person but an old man who liked to sit in the sun and do absolutely nothing. But he was careful not to let this be known for fear the King would cut off his head.

The King lived in a palace made entirely of crystal. In the early days of his reign it had shone so brightly that passers-by would hide their eyes, for fear of being dazzled. But gradually the crystal grew duller and the dust of the seasons covered its brightness. Nobody could be spared to polish it for everyone was far too busy helping the King think his thoughts. At any moment they might be ordered to leave their work and hurry away on the King's business. To China, perhaps, to count the silkworms. Or to find out if the Solomon Islands were ruled by the Queen of Sheba. When they came back with their lists of facts, the King and the courtiers would write them down in large books bound in leather. And if anyone returned without an answer, his head was at once cut off.

The only person in the palace who had nothing to do was the Queen. All day long she sat on her golden throne, twisting the necklace of blue-and-green flowers that was clasped about her throat. Sometimes she would start up with a cry and pull her ermine robes about her. For the palace, as it grew more and more dirty, became infested with mice. And mice, as anyone will tell you, are the things no Queen can stand.

"O-o-o-h!" she would say, with a little gasp, as she leapt on the seat of the throne.

And each time she cried out the King would frown.

"Silence please!" he would say, in a fractious voice, for the least little noise disturbed his thinking. Then the mice would scatter for a little while and no sound would be heard in the room. Except for the scratching of goose-quill pens as the King and the courtiers added new facts to the ones in the leather books.

The Queen never gave orders, not even to her Ladies-of-the-Bedchamber. For as likely as not the King would countermand them.

"Mend the Queen's petticoat?" he would say crossly. "What petticoat? Why waste time talking about petticoats? Take a pen and write out these facts about the Phoenix!"

What a dreadful state of affairs, you will say! And, indeed, I wouldn't blame you. But you must not think it was always like that. The Queen, sitting lonely upon her throne, would often remind herself of the days when she first had married the King. How tall and handsome he had been, with his strong white neck and ruddy cheeks, and locks of hair folded round his head like the leaves of camellia flowers.

"Ah!" she would sigh, remembering back. How he had fed her with honey-cakes and fingers of buttered bread from his plate. How his face had been so full of love that her heart would turn over in her breast and force her to look away, for sheer joy.

But at last there came a fateful evening.

"Your eyes are brighter than stars," he said, as he glanced from her face to the shining sky. But instead of turning to her again as usual, he continued to gaze upwards.

"I wonder," he said dreamily, "just how many stars there are! I think I shall count them. One, two, three, four, five, six, seven —— " And he went on counting till the Queen fell asleep beside him.

"One thousand, two hundred and forty-nine —— " he was saying as she woke up.

And after that he would not be satisfied till he got the courtiers out of their beds and set them to counting stars. And as no two answers came out alike the King was very angry.

That was how it all began.

The next day, the King exclaimed, "Your cheeks, my Darling, are like two roses!"

And the Queen was very happy till he added, "But why roses? Why not cabbages? Why are cheeks pink and cabbages green? And vice versa? This is a very serious question."

The third day he told her that her teeth were like pearls. But before she even had time to smile, he went on ——

"And what if they are? Everybody has, after all, a certain number of teeth, and most of them are pearly. Pearls themselves, however, are very rare. It is more important to think about them."

So he summoned the best divers in the kingdom and sent them down under the sea.

And from that day onwards he was always thinking. He was only concerned with gaining knowledge and he never even looked at the Queen. Indeed, if he had glanced in her direction, he would probably not have seen her, for he worked so hard at his books and papers that he soon became very short-sighted. His round red face grew thin and wrinkled, and his hair turned grey at an early age. He ate practically nothing — except for a cheese-and-onion sandwich whenever the old Prime Minister told him that dinner was on the table.

Well! You can imagine how lonely the Queen was. Sometimes the Prime Minister would shuffle cautiously to the throne and pat her hand kindly. Sometimes the little page who filled the inkwells would raise his eyes and smile at her from behind the King's back. But neither the old man nor the boy could spare much time to amuse the Queen, for fear of losing their heads.

You must not think the King meant to be unkind. Indeed, it seemed to him that his subjects were luckier than most, for hadn't they a King who knew practically everything? But while he was busy gathering knowledge his people grew poorer and poorer. Houses fell into ruin and fields went untilled, because the King needed all the men to help him in his thinking.

At last there came a day when the King and the courtiers were busy, as usual, at their desks in the Council Chamber. The Queen sat listening to the scratching of pens and the squeaking of mice in the wainscot. And presently, as she sat so still, a bold mouse streaked across the floor and began to wash its whiskers right under the throne. The Queen gave a little frightened gasp. But she quickly clapped her hand to her mouth for fear of disturbing the King. Then she pulled her ermine train about her and sat trembling within it. And at that moment, over the edge of her hand, her startled eyes glanced across the room and saw on the threshold — a cat.

A small cat it was, as fluffy as a dandelion, and white as sugar from tail to whisker. It walked with a lazy swinging step as though it had nothing at all to do and all time to do it in. A pair of green eyes glowed in its head as it sauntered through the door.

For a moment it paused at the carpet's edge, glancing curiously at the King and the courtiers as they bent above their books. Then the green eyes turned towards the Queen. The Cat gave a start and its body stiffened. Up went its back like the hump of a camel. Its whiskers stretched into threads of steel. Then it leapt across the Council Chamber and dived beneath the throne. There was a hoarse cat-cry. And a smothered squeak. And the mouse was there no longer.

"Silence, please! Don't make such extraordinary noises,

my dear! They interrupt my thoughts!" said the King frac-
tiously.

"It wasn't me," said the Queen timidly. "It was a Cat."

"Cats?" said the King absent-mindedly, without even
lifting his head. "Cats are four-footed creatures covered
with fur. They eat mice, fish, liver and birds and com-
municate either in a purr or a caterwaul. They keep
themselves to themselves and are popularly supposed to
possess nine lives. For further information on Cats, see
Page Two, Volume Seven, Shelf D in Library Number
Five to the left as you go in the door. Here! Hi! What's
all this —— ?"

With a start the King looked up from his page. For the
Cat was sitting on the desk before him.

"Kindly be careful!" the King said crossly. "You're right
on my latest facts. They deal with a very important question. Do turkeys really come from Turkey and if not, why?
Well, what do you want? Speak up! Don't mumble."

"I want to have a look at you," the Cat said calmly.

"Oho! You do, do you? Well, a Cat may look at a King,
they say! And I've no objection. Go ahead!"

The King leaned backwards in his chair and turned his
face from left to right so the Cat could see both sides.

The Cat gazed thoughtfully at the King.

There was a long pause.

"Well?" said the King, with a tolerant smile. "And what
do you think of me, may I ask?"

The Cat was sitting on the desk before him

"Not much," said the Cat casually, licking its right front paw.

"What?" cried the King. "Not much, indeed! My poor ignorant animal, you are evidently not aware *which* King you are looking at!"

"All kings are pretty much alike," said the Cat.

"Nothing of the kind," the King said angrily. "I defy you to name a single king that knows as much as I do. Why, professors come from the ends of the earth to consult with me for half an hour. My court is composed of the Very Best People. Jack-the-Giant-Killer digs my garden. My flocks are tended by no less a person than Bo-Peep. And all my pies contain Four-and-Twenty Blackbirds. Not much to look at, forsooth! And who are you, I'd like to know, to speak to a King like that!"

"Oh, just a cat," the Cat replied. "Four legs and a tail and a couple of whiskers."

"I can see that for myself!" snapped the King. "It doesn't matter to me what you *look* like. What *I* care about is, how much do you know?"

"Oh, everything," the Cat said calmly, as it licked the tip of its tail.

"What!" The King burst out with an angry splutter. "Well, of all the vain, conceited creatures! I've a jolly good mind to chop off your head."

"So you shall," said the Cat. "But all in good time."

"Everything! Why, you preposterous animal! There's

no one alive — not even myself — who could be as wise as that!"

"With the single exception of cats," said the Cat. "All cats, I assure you, know everything!"

"Very well," growled the King. "But you've got to prove it. If you're so clever I shall ask you three questions. And then we shall see what we'll see."

He smiled a supercilious smile. If the wretched Cat insisted on boasting, it would have to take the consequences!

"Now," he said, leaning back in his chair and putting his fingers together. "My first question is ——"

"One moment, please!" the Cat said calmly. "I cannot undertake to answer your questions until we have settled the terms. No cat would do anything so foolish. I am prepared to make a bargain with you. And these are my conditions. It is agreed between us that you shall ask me three questions. After that, it is only fair that I should question you. And whichever one of us wins the contest shall have command of your kingdom."

The courtiers dropped their pens in surprise. The King's eyes goggled with astonishment.

But he swallowed the words that sprang to his mouth and gave a disdainful laugh.

"Very well," he said haughtily. "It's a great waste of time and you, not I, will be the one to regret it. But I accept your bargain."

"Then take off your crown," commanded the Cat, "and lay it on the table between us."

The King tore the crown from his tattered head and the jewels flashed in the sunlight.

"Let's get this nonsense over and done with! I have to go on with my work," he said crossly. "Are you ready? Well, here is my first question. If you laid them carefully, end to end, how many six-foot men would it take to go right round the Equator?"

"That's easy," the Cat replied, with a smile. "You simply divide the length by six."

"Aha!" cried the King with a crafty look. "That's all very well — but what *is* the length?"

"Any length you like," the Cat said airily. "It doesn't really exist, you know. The Equator is purely an imaginary line."

The King's face darkened with disapproval.

"Well," he said sulkily, "tell me this. What is the difference between an Elephant and a Railway Porter?"

"No difference at all," said the Cat at once. "Because they both carry trunks."

"But — but — but — but ——" the King protested. "These are not the answers I expected. You really must try to be more serious."

"I can't help what you expected," said the Cat. "These are the proper replies to your questions, as any cat will tell you."

The King made an angry click with his tongue.

"This nonsense is getting beyond a joke! It's a farce! It's nothing but twiddle-twaddle. Well, here is my third question — *if* you can answer it."

You could see by the smile on the King's face that *this* time he thought he had the Cat exactly where he wanted it.

He held up a pompous hand and began.

"If a dozen men, working eight hours a day, had to dig a hole ten-and-a-half miles deep — how long would it be, including Sundays, before they put down their spades?"

The King's eyes shone with a cunning sparkle. He gazed at the Cat with a look of triumph. But the Cat had its answer ready.

"Two seconds," it said quickly, with a little flick of its tail.

"Two seconds! Are you mad? The answer's in years!" The King rubbed his hands together with glee at the thought of the Cat's mistake.

"I repeat," said the Cat. "It would take them two seconds. To dig such a hole would be utterly foolish. 'Ten miles deep?' they would say. 'Why, what on earth for?' "

"That isn't the point," the King said angrily.

"But every question must have a point. A point is exactly what questions are for. And now," said the Cat, "it's my turn, I believe!"

The King gave an angry shrug of his shoulders.

"Well, be quick. You've wasted enough of my time!"

"My questions are short and very simple," the Cat assured him. "A cat could solve them in a flick of the whisker. Let us hope that a King will be equally clever. Now, here is my first. How high is the sky?"

The King gave a grunt of satisfaction. This was exactly the kind of question he liked, and he smiled a knowing smile.

"Well, of course," he began, "it all depends. If you measured it from a level plain it would be one height. From the top of a mountain another. And after taking this into account, we should have to determine the latitude and longitude, the amplitude, magnitude and multitude, not forgetting the atmospherics, mathematics, acrobatics and hysterics; and the general depressions, expressions, impressions and confessions, together with —— "

"Excuse me," interrupted the Cat. "But that is not the answer. Try again, please. How high is the sky?"

The King's eyes popped with angry astonishment. Nobody had ever dared to interrupt him before.

"The sky," he bellowed, "is — er — it's —— . Well, of course I can't tell you in so many yards. Neither could anyone else, I assure you. It is probably —— "

"I want an exact reply," said the Cat. He glanced from the King to the gaping courtiers. "Has anyone here, in this hall of learning, the answer to my question?"

Nervously glancing at the King, the Prime Minister raised a trembling hand.

"I have always supposed," he murmured shyly, "that the sky was just a little higher than the Eagle flies. I'm an old man, of course, and I'm probably wrong ———— "

The Cat clapped its sugar-white paws together.

"No! No! You are right," it protested gently.

The King gave a sullen snort of rage.

"Tomfoolery! Nonsensical bosh!"

The Cat held up its paw for silence. "Will you answer my second question, please! Where is the sweetest milk to be found?"

Immediately the King's face cleared, and took on a confident smirk.

"As simple as A.B.C.," he said loftily. "The answer, of course, is Sardinia. For there the cows live on honey and roses and their milk is as sweet as Golden Syrup. Or perhaps I should say the Elegant Islands, where they feed upon nothing but sugar cane. Or Greece, where they browse in the Candytuft. Now, taking into consideration ———— "

"I can take nothing into consideration," said the Cat, "except the fact that you have not answered my question. Where is the sweetest milk, O King?"

"I know!" cried the little Page, pausing for a moment above a half-filled inkwell. "In a saucer by the fire."

The Cat gave the child an approving nod and yawned in the face of the King.

"I thought you were so clever!" it said slyly. "You may indeed be the wisest of Kings — but somebody else has

answered my question. Do not frown, however — " for
the King was glowering at the Page — "you still have one
more chance to win. Here is my third question. What is
the strongest thing in the world?"

The King's eyes glittered. This time he was certain he
had the right answer.

"The Tiger," he said thoughtfully, "is a very strong
thing. So also are the Horse and the Lion. Then, of course,
there are the tides of the sea. And the granite veins of the
mountains. Volcanoes, too, have a mighty strength and the
snowy caps of ice at the Poles. Or, again, it might be the
Wall of China — — "

"Or again it might not!" the Cat broke in. "Can anyone
tell me the strongest thing?"

It glanced once more round the Council Chamber. And
this time it was the Queen who spoke.

"I think," she said gently, "it must be Patience. For, in
the long run, it is Patience that overcomes all things."

The green eyes dwelt gravely upon her for a moment.

"It is indeed," the Cat agreed quietly. And turning, it
laid a paw on the crown.

"Oh, wisest of monarchs!" cried the Cat. "You are, without doubt, a mighty scholar and I am a common-or-garden
cat. But I have answered all three of your questions and
you have not answered one of mine. The result of the contest is clear, I think. The crown belongs to me."

The King gave a short contemptuous laugh.

"Don't be so silly! What would you do with it? You can't make laws and rule the people. You don't even know how to read or write. Turn over my kingdom to a Cat? I'm hanged if I will!"

The Cat smiled broadly.

"I see that your wisdom does not include a knowledge of fairy-tales. If it did, you would know that it is only necessary to cut off a cat's head to discover a Prince in disguise."

"Fairy-tales? Pooh! They're nothing to me. I'm thinking about my kingdom."

"Your kingdom," said the Cat, "if you'll forgive me mentioning it, is no longer your affair. All that need concern you now is quickly to cut off my head. The rest you may leave to me. Furthermore, since you apparently have no use for them, I shall take into my service this wise man, your Prime Minister, this understanding woman, your wife, and this sensible child, your page. Let them get their hats and come with me and together we four shall rule the kingdom."

"But what's going to happen to *me*?" cried the King. "Where shall I go? How shall I live?"

The Cat's eyes narrowed sternly.

"You should have thought of that before. Most people think twice before making a bargain with a Cat. Well, out with your sword now, learned man! And I trust the blade is sharp."

"Stop!" cried the Prime Minister, as he laid his hand on

the hilt of the King's sword. Then he turned to the Cat and bowed respectfully.

"Sir," he said quietly, "listen to me! It is true that you have won the crown, in fair and equal contest. And it may be you are indeed a Prince. But I must decline your offer. I have served the King faithfully since the days when I was a page in his father's court. And whether he be crowned or uncrowned, head of a kingdom or a tramp on the lonely roads, I love him and he needs me. I will not go with you."

"Nor I," said the Queen, as she rose from her golden throne. "I have stood at the King's side since he was young and comely. I have waited for him in silence through long, lonely years. Whether he be wise or foolish, rich or without bread, I love him and I need him. I will not go with you."

"Nor I," said the little Page, as he corked up his bottle of ink. "This is the only home I have ever known. And the King is my king and I am sorry for him. Besides, I like filling up the inkwells. I will not go with you."

At that the Cat smiled a curious smile and its green eyes shone on the three who had refused him.

"What have you to say to this, O King?" said the Cat as it turned to the desk.

But no words came to answer the question. For the King was weeping.

"O wise man, why do you weep?" asked the Cat.

"Because I am ashamed," sobbed the King. "I boasted about how clever I was. I thought I knew everything — pretty nearly. And now I find that an old man and a woman and a little lad are all far wiser than I am. Do not try to comfort me!" he wept, as the Queen and the Prime Minister touched his hands. "I am not worth it. I know nothing at all. Not even who I am!"

He hid his face in the crook of his arm. "Oh, I know that I'm a King!" he cried. "I know my name and address, of course! But I do not know, after all these years, who I really, truly am!"

"Look at me and you will find out," said the Cat quietly.

"But I h-h-have looked at you!" sobbed the King into his handkerchief.

"Not really," the Cat insisted gently. "You have only glanced at me, now and again. A Cat may look at a King you say. But a King may also look at a Cat. If you did that, you would know who you are. Look in my eyes — and see!"

The King took his face out of the handkerchief and peered at the Cat through his tears. His eyes wandered over the calm white face and came at last to the Cat's green eyes. Within that shining, piercing gaze he saw his own reflection.

"Closer. Closer," the Cat commanded.

Obediently the King bent nearer.

And as he gazed at those fathomless eyes, a change came over the man within them. Slowly, his thin, pinched face grew fatter. The pale cheeks plumped into round red pouches and the wrinkles smoothed themselves out of his brow. Bright locks of brown curled upon his head; a brown beard sprang from his greying chin. The King gave a start of surprise and smiled. And a big broad rosy man smiled back from the mirroring eyes of the Cat.

"My Glorious Ghosts! That's *me!*" he cried. "I know who I really am at last! Why, *I'm* not the cleverest man in the world!" He flung up his head with a gusty laugh. "Ho-ho! Ha-ha! I see it all now! I'm not a thinking person at all. I'm nothing but a Merry Old Soul!"

He waved his arms at the gaping courtiers. "Here, you! Take away those pens and papers. Tear up the notebooks! Bury the desks! And if anyone mentions a fact to me I shall cut off his head myself!"

He gave another uproarious laugh and embraced the Prime Minister so tightly that he nearly killed the old man.

"Forgive me, my faithful friend!" he cried. "And bring me my Pipe and a Bowl of Punch and call in my Fiddlers Three!"

"And you, my Joy, my Treasure, my Dove——" he turned to the Queen with outstretched arms. "Oh, give me your hand again, dear heart, and I'll never let it go!"

Happy tears crept down the cheeks of the Queen, and the King touched them gently away. "I don't need stars in the sky," he whispered, "I have them here, in your eyes."

"Forgive me if I interrupt. But what about me?" exclaimed the Cat.

"Well, you've got the kingdom. You've got the crown! What more do you want?" the King demanded.

"Pooh!" said the Cat. "They're no use to me! Accept them, I pray, as a friendly gift. But as no cat ever gives something for nothing, I demand in return two small re-quests ——"

"Oh, anything. Anything at all," said the King with a lordly gesture.

"I should like, every now and then," said the Cat, "to come to the Palace and see ——"

"Me? Why, of course! You're always welcome!" The King broke in with a satisfied smile.

"To see the Queen," the Cat continued, ignoring the King's remark.

"Oh — the Queen! All right. Whenever you like. You can help us to keep down the mice."

"My second request," the Cat went on, "is the little chain of blue-and-green flowers that the Queen wears round her neck."

"Take it — and welcome!" the King said airily. "It was only a cheap one, anyway."

Slowly the Queen put up her hands and unfastened the clasp at her throat. She twined the necklace about the Cat, looping it round the furry body and over and under the tail. Then for a long moment she looked deep into the Cat's green eyes and the Cat looked into hers. And in that look lay all the secrets that Queens and cats carry in their hearts and never tell to anyone.

"My At Home days are every Second Friday," said the Queen, as she smiled at the Cat.

"I shall come," the Cat said nodding.

And having said that, he turned away and, without a glance at anyone else, sailed out of the Council Chamber. The blue-and-green necklace shone in his fur and his tail waved to and fro like a banner.

"By the way!" called the King, as the Cat departed. "Are you sure you're really a prince in disguise? Could I have safely cut off your head?"

The Cat turned about and regarded him gravely. Then it smiled its mocking smile.

"Nothing is certain in this world. Good-bye!" said the green-eyed Cat.

It sprang across the sunny threshold and down the Castle steps.

On the Palace lawn a red cow was admiring her reflection in an ornamental pond.

"Who are you?" she enquired, as the Cat passed by.

"I'm the Cat that Looked at a King," he replied.

"And I," she remarked with a toss of her head, "am the Cow that Jumped Over the Moon."

"Is that so?" said the Cat. "Whatever for?"

The Cow stared. She had never before been asked that question. And suddenly it occurred to her that there might be something else to do than jumping over moons.

"Now that you mention it," she said shyly, "I don't think I really know." And she trotted away across the lawn to think the matter over.

On the garden path a large grey bird was noisily flapping its wings.

"I'm the Goose that Lays the Golden Eggs!" it quacked haughtily.

"Indeed?" said the Cat, "and where are your goslings?"

"Goslings?" The Goose turned a trifle pale. "Well, now that you mention it, I have none. I always felt there was something missing." And she hurried off to make a nest and lay a common egg.

Plop! A green shape dropped in front of the Cat.

"I'm the Frog that Would a-Wooing Go," it said proudly.

"Do you tell me that, now?" the Cat said gravely. "Well, I trust you are happily married."

"Er —— now that you mention it — not exactly. In fact — er — no!" confessed the Frog.

"Ah," said the Cat, with a shake of his head. "You should have obeyed your Mother!"

And before the Frog could do more than blink, the Cat had passed on. Away he went down the garden path, his whiskers twitching in the morning air, his blue-and-green necklace shining in the sun and his white tail waving like a banner behind him.

And as he disappeared through the Palace gates, all those who had seen him felt rich and happy.

The Cow and the Goose and the Frog were happy for now they could stop doing foolish things that had no rhyme or reason. The courtiers all were happy men, dancing by day to the Fiddlers' tunes and drinking at night from the flowing Bowl. The King himself was extremely happy because he no longer thought about anything. And the Queen was happy for a very good reason — because the King was happy. The little Page was happy, too. For now he could fill the inkwells with ink, and empty them back in the bottle again with no one to say him nay. But the happiest person in all the world was the old Prime Minister.

Do you know what he did?

He issued a proclamation.

The King commanded his subjects (it said) to put up Maypoles and dance around them; to get out Merry-go-rounds and ride them; to dance and feast and sing and grow fat and love one another dearly. And, furthermore, (it was clearly printed) if anyone disobeyed these laws, the King would immediately cut off his head.

And, having done that, the Prime Minister felt he had done enough. He spent the rest of his days doing nothing — just sitting in the sun in a rocking-chair, making himself a gentle breeze with a fan of cocoanut palm.

As for the Cat, he went his way through the ways of the world, decked in the Queen's bright necklace; and gazing at everything he saw with his green and piercing eyes.

He is still wandering, some folks say, for Near and Far are alike to him. And always as he goes, he watches out for one or another who will return his gaze. A king, it may be, or perhaps a shepherd, or a man going by through the city streets. If he comes upon anyone like that, he will stay with them for a little while. Not very long, but long enough. It takes no more than the tick of a second to look down deep in his deep green eyes and discover who they are. . . .

The dreamy voice was hushed and silent. The sunlight crept away from the window and dusk came slowly in. Not a sound could be heard in the Nursery but the ticking of the clock.

Then, with a start, as though she were coming back from a great distance, Mary Poppins turned to the children. Her eyes snapped angrily.

"May I ask what you're doing out of bed? I thought you were dying of toothache, Michael! What are you gaping at me for, Jane? I am not a Performing Bear!"

And, snatching up her wool, she became her usual whirlwind self.

With a squeak, Michael hurled himself into bed. But Jane did not move.

"I wonder who I am!" she said softly, half to herself and half to Michael.

"I *know* who I am," said Michael stoutly. "I'm Michael George Banks, of Cherry-Tree Lane. And I don't need a Cat to tell me."

"He doesn't need anyone to tell him anything. Clever Mr. Smarty!" Mary Poppins tossed him a scornful smile.

"When he comes back," Jane murmured slowly, "I shall look right into his deep green eyes!"

"You and your deep green eyes, indeed! Better look into your own black face and see that it's clean for Supper!" Mary Poppins sniffed her usual sniff.

"Perhaps he won't come back!" said Michael. A Cat that

could look at a King, he thought, would hardly want to spend its days on the top of a mantelpiece.

"Oh, yes, he will — won't he, Mary Poppins?" Jane's voice was full of anxiety.

"How should I know?" snapped Mary Poppins. "I'm not a Public Library!"

"But it's Michael's cat —— " Jane began to argue, when Mrs. Banks' voice interrupted her.

"Mary Poppins!" it called from the foot of the stairs. "Could you possibly spare me a moment?"

The children looked at each other questioningly. Their Mother's voice was shrill with alarm. Mary Poppins hurried out of the room. Michael pushed the blankets away once more and crept with Jane to the top of the stairs.

Down in the front hall Mr. Banks sat huddled upon a chair. Mrs. Banks was anxiously stroking his head and giving him sips of water.

"He seems to have had some kind of shock," she explained to Mary Poppins. "Can't you tell us, George, exactly what happened? Whatever can be the matter?"

Mr. Banks raised a ghostly face. "A Nervous Breakdown — that's what's the matter. I'm overworking. I'm seeing things."

"What things?" demanded Mrs. Banks.

Mr. Banks took a sip of water.

"I was turning in at the end of the Lane when —— " he

gave a shudder and closed his eyes. "I saw it standing right by our gate."

"You saw what standing?" cried Mrs. Banks frantically.

"A white thing. Sort of leopard it was. And forget-me-nots growing all over its fur. When I got to the gate it — looked at me. A wild green look — right into my eyes. Then it nodded and said 'Good-evening, Banks!' and hurried up the path."

"But —— " Mrs. Banks began to argue.

Mr. Banks raised a protesting hand.

"I know what you're going to say. Well, don't. The leopards are all locked up in the Zoo. And they don't have forget-me-nots on them, anyway. I'm perfectly well aware of that. But it just goes to show that I'm very ill. You'd better send for Dr. Simpson."

Mrs. Banks ran to the telephone. And a stifled hiccup came from the landing.

"What's the matter with you up there?" asked Mr. Banks faintly.

But Jane and Michael could not answer. They were overcome by a storm of giggles. They writhed and rolled and rocked on the floor and gulped and gurgled with laughter.

For while Mr. Banks was describing his shock, a white shape had appeared at the Nursery window. Lightly it leapt from the sill to the floor and up to its place on the mantelpiece. It sat there now with its tail curled round it and its whiskers folded against its cheeks. Dappled with small, blue, shining flowers, its green eyes gazing across the room, silent and still on the mantelpiece, sat Michael's China Cat.

"Well, of all the hard-hearted, unfeeling children!" Mr. Banks stared up at them, shocked and hurt.

But that only made them laugh more loudly. They giggled and coughed and choked and exploded till Mary Poppins bent back her head and fixed them with one of her fiercest glares.

Then there was silence. Not even a hiccup. For that look, as Jane and Michael knew, was enough to stop anyone laughing. . . .

CHAPTER FOUR

The Marble Boy

nd don't forget to buy me an evening paper!" said Mrs. Banks, as she handed Jane two pennies and kissed her good-bye.

Michael looked at his Mother reproachfully.

"Is that all you're going to give us?" he asked. "What'll happen if we meet the Ice Cream Man?"

"Well," said Mrs. Banks reluctantly. "Here's another sixpence. But I do think you children get too many treats. *I* didn't have Ices every day when *I* was a little girl."

Michael looked at her curiously. He could not believe she had ever been a little girl. Mrs. George Banks in short skirts and her hair tied up with ribbons? Impossible!

"I suppose," he said smugly, "you didn't deserve them!"

And he tucked the sixpence carefully into the pocket of his sailor suit.

"That's Fourpence for the Ice Creams," said Jane. "And we'll buy a *Lot-o'-Fun,* with the rest."

"Out of my way, Miss, if you please!" said a haughty voice behind her.

As neat and trim as a fashion-plate, Mary Poppins came down the steps with Annabel. She dumped her into the perambulator and pushed it past the children.

"Now, Quick March into the Park!" she snapped. "And no meandering!"

Down the path straggled Jane and Michael, with John and Barbara at their heels. The sun spread over Cherry-Tree Lane like a bright enormous umbrella. Thrushes and blackbirds sang in the trees. Down at the corner Admiral Boom was busily mowing his lawn.

From the distance came sounds of martial music. The Band was playing at the end of the Park. Along the walks went the flowery sunshades and beneath them sauntered gossiping ladies, exchanging the latest news.

The Park Keeper, in his summer suit — blue with a red stripe on the sleeve — was keeping an eye on everyone as he tramped across the lawns.

"Observe the Rules! Keep Off the Grass! All Litter to be Placed in the Baskets!" he shouted.

Jane gazed at the sunny, dreamy scene. "It's just like Mr. Twigley's box," she said with a happy sigh.

Michael put his ear to the trunk of an oak.

"I believe I can hear it growing!" he cried. "It makes a small, soft, creeping sound ——"

"*You'll* be creeping in a minute! Right back home, un-less you hurry!" Mary Poppins warned him.

"No Rubbish Allowed in the Park!" shouted the Keeper, as she swept along the Lime Walk.

"Rubbish yourself!" she retorted briskly, with a haughty toss of her head.

He took off his hat and fanned his face as he stared at her retreating back. And you knew from the way Mary Poppins smiled that she knew quite well he was staring. How could he help it, she thought to herself. Wasn't she wearing her new white jacket, with the pink collar and the pink belt and the four pink buttons down the front?

"Which way are we going today?" asked Michael.

"That remains to be seen!" she answered him priggishly.

"I was only enquiring —— " Michael argued.

"Don't, then!" she advised, with a warning sniff.

"She never lets me say anything!" he grumbled under his hat to Jane. "I'll go dumb some day and then she'll be sorry!"

Mary Poppins thrust the perambulator in front of her as though she were running an obstacle race.

"This way, please!" she commanded presently, as she swung the pram to the right.

And they knew, then, where they were going. For the little path that turned out of the Lime Walk led away to-wards the Lake.

There, beyond the tunnels of shade, lay the shining patch of water. It sparkled and danced in its net of sunlight and the children felt their hearts beat faster as they ran through the shadows towards it.

"I'll make a boat, and sail it to Africa!" shouted Michael, forgetting his crossness.

"I'll go fishing!" cried Jane, as she galloped past him.

Laughing and whooping and waving their hats, they came to the shining water. All round the Lake stood the dusty green benches, and the ducks went quacking along the edge, greedily looking for crusts.

At the far end of the water stood the battered marble statue of the Boy and the Dolphin. Dazzling white and bright it shone, between the Lake and the sky. There was a

small chip off the Boy's nose and a line like a black thread round his ankle. One of the fingers of his left hand was broken off at the joint. And all his toes were cracked.

There he stood, on his high pedestal, with his arm flung lightly round the neck of the Dolphin. His head, with its ruffle of marble curls, was bent towards the water. He gazed down at it thoughtfully with wide marble eyes. The name NELEUS was carved in faded gilt letters at the base of the pedestal.

"How bright he is today!" breathed Jane, blinking her eyes at the shining marble.

And it was at that moment that she saw the Elderly Gentleman.

He was sitting at the foot of the statue, reading a book

with the aid of a magnifying glass. His bald head was sheltered from the sun by a knotted silk handkerchief, and lying on the bench beside him was a black top-hat.

The children stared at the curious figure with fascinated eyes.

"That's Mary Poppins' favourite seat! She *will* be cross!" exclaimed Michael.

"Indeed? And when was I ever cross?" her voice enquired behind him.

The remark quite shocked him. "Why, you're *often* cross, Mary Poppins!" he said. "At least fifty times a day!"

"Never!" she said with an angry snap. "I have the patience of a Boa Constrictor! I merely Speak My Mind!"

She flounced away and sat down on a bench exactly opposite the Statue. Then she glared across the Lake at the Elderly Gentleman. It was a look that might have killed anybody else. But the Elderly Gentleman was quite unaffected. He went on poring over his book and took no notice of anyone. Mary Poppins, with an infuriated sniff, took her mending-bag from the perambulator and began to darn the socks.

The children scattered round the sparkling water.

"Here's my boat!" shrieked Michael, snatching a piece of coloured paper from a litter basket.

"I'm fishing," said Jane, as she lay on her stomach and stretched her hand over the water. She imagined a fishing-rod in her fingers and a line running down, with a hook and a worm. After a little while, she knew, a fish would swim lazily up to the hook and give the worm a tweak. Then, with a jerk, she would land him neatly and take him home in her hat. "Well, I never!" Mrs. Brill would say. "It's just what we needed for supper!"

Beside her the Twins were happily paddling. Michael steered his ship through a terrible storm. Mary Poppins sat primly on her bench and rocked the perambulator with one foot. Her silver needle flashed in the sunlight. The Park was quiet and dreamy and still.

Bang!

The Elderly Gentleman closed his book and the sound shattered the silence.

"Oh, I say!" protested a shrill sweet voice. "You might have let me finish!"

Jane and Michael looked up in surprise. They stared. They blinked. And they stared again. For there, on the grass before them, stood the little marble statue. The marble Dolphin was clasped in his arms and the pedestal was quite empty.

The Elderly Gentleman opened his mouth. Then he shut it and opened it again.

"Er — did you say something?" he said at last, and his eyebrows went up to the top of his head.

"Yes, of course I did!" the Boy replied. "I was reading over your shoulder there — — " he pointed towards the empty pedestal, "and you closed the book too quickly. I wanted to finish the Elephant story and see how he got his Trunk."

"Oh, I *beg* your pardon," said the Elderly Gentleman. "I had no idea — er — of such a thing. I always stop reading at four, you see. I have to get home to my Tea."

He rose and folded the handkerchief and picked up the black top hat.

"Well, now that you've finished," the Boy said calmly, "you can give the book to me!"

The Elderly Gentleman drew back, clutching the book to his breast.

"Oh, I couldn't do that, I'm afraid," he said. "You see, I've only just bought it. I wanted to read it when I was young, but the grown-ups always got it first. And now that I've got a copy of my own, I really feel I must keep it."

He eyed the statue uneasily as though he feared that at any moment it might snatch the book away.

"*I* could tell you about the Elephant's Child —— " Jane murmured shyly to the Boy.

He wheeled around with the fish in his arms.

"Oh, Jane — would you really?" he cried in surprise. His marble face gleamed with pleasure.

"And I'll tell you *Yellow Dog Dingo*," said Michael, "and *The Butterfly That Stamped*."

"No!" said the Elderly Gentleman suddenly. "Here am I with a suit of clothes and a hat. And he's quite naked. I'll *give* him the book! I suppose," he added, with a gloomy sigh, "I was never meant to have it."

He gave the book a last long look, and, thrusting it at the Marble Boy, he turned away quickly. But the Dolphin wriggled and caught his eye and he turned to the Boy again.

"By the way," he said, curiously, "I wonder how you caught that Porpoise? What did you use — a line or a net?"

"Neither," replied the Boy, with a smile. "He was given to me when I was born."

"Oh — I see." The Elderly Gentleman nodded, though he still looked rather puzzled. "Well — I must be getting along. Good-day!" He lifted the black top-hat politely and hurried off down the path.

"Thank you!" the Marble Boy shouted after him, as he eagerly opened the book. On the fly-leaf was written, in spidery writing, "*William Weatherall Wilkins.*"

"I'll cross out his name and put mine instead." The Boy smiled gaily at Jane and Michael.

"But what is your name? And how can you read?" cried Michael, very astonished.

"My name is Neleus," the Boy said laughing. "And I read with my eyes, of course!"

"But you're only a statue!" Jane protested. "And statues don't usually walk and talk. However did you get down?"

"I jumped," replied Neleus, smiling again, as he tossed

his marble curls. "I was so disappointed not to finish that story, that something happened to my feet. First they twitched, and then they jumped and the next thing I knew I was down on the grass!" He curled his little marble toes and stamped on the earth with his marble feet. "Oh, lucky, lucky human beings to be able to do this every day! I've watched you so often, Jane and Michael, and wished I could come and play with you. And now at last my wish has come true. Oh, tell me you're glad to see me!"

He touched their cheeks with his marble fingers and crowed with joy as he danced around them. Then before

they could utter a word of welcome he sped like a hare to the edge of the Lake and dabbled his hand in the water.

"So — this is what water feels like!" he cried. "So deep and so blue — and as light as air!" He leaned out over the sparkling Lake and the Dolphin gave a flick of its tail and slipped from his arms with a splash.

"Catch him! He'll sink!" cried Michael quickly.

But the Dolphin did nothing of the kind. It swam round the Lake and threshed the water; it dived and caught its tail in its mouth and leapt in the air and dived again. The performance was just like a turn in the circus. And as it sprang, dripping, to the arms of its master, the children could not help clapping.

"Was it good?" asked Neleus enviously. And the Dolphin grinned and nodded.

"Good!" cried a well-known voice behind them. "I call it extremely naughty!"

Mary Poppins was standing at the edge of the Lake and her eyes were as bright as her darning needle. Neleus sprang to his feet with a little cry and hung his head before her. He looked very young and small and shy as he waited for her to speak.

"Who said you might get down, may I ask?" Her face had its usual look of fury.

He shook his head guiltily.

"No one," he mumbled. "My feet jumped down by themselves, Mary Poppins."

"Then they'd better jump up again, spit-spot. You've no right to be off your pedestal."

He tilted back his marble head and the sunlight glanced off his small chipped nose.

"Oh, can't I stay down, Mary Poppins?" he pleaded. "Do let me stay for a little while and play with Jane and Michael! You don't know how lonely it is up there, with only the birds to talk to!" The earnest marble eyes entreated her. "Please, Mary Poppins!" he whispered softly, as he clasped his marble hands.

She gazed down thoughtfully for a moment, as though she were making up her mind. Then her eyes softened. A little smile skipped over her mouth and crinkled the edge of her cheek.

"Well, just for this afternoon!" she said. "This one time, Neleus! Never again!"

"Never — I promise, Mary Poppins!" He gave her an impish grin.

"Do you know Mary Poppins?" demanded Michael. "Where did you meet her?" he wanted to know. He was feeling a little jealous.

"Of course I do!" exclaimed Neleus laughing. "She's a very old friend of my Father's."

"What is your Father's name? Where is he?" Jane was almost bursting with curiosity.

"Far away. In the Isles of Greece. He is called the King of

the Sea." As he spoke, the marble eyes of Neleus brimmed slowly up with sadness.

"What does he do?" demanded Michael. "Does he go to the City — like Daddy?"

"Oh, no! He never goes anywhere. He stands on a cliff above the sea, holding his trident and blowing his horn. Beside him my Mother sits, combing her hair. And Pelias, that's my younger brother, plays at their feet with a marble shell. And all day long the gulls fly past them, making black shadows on their marble bodies, and telling them news of the harbour. By day they watch the red-sailed ships going in and out of the bay. And at night they listen to the wine-dark waters that break on the shore below."

"How lovely!" cried Jane. "But why did you leave them?"

She was thinking that she would never have left Mr. and Mrs. Banks and Michael alone on the cliffs of Greece.

"I didn't want to," said the Marble Boy. "But what can a statue do against men? They were always coming to stare at us — peeking and prying and pinching our arms. They said we were made a long time ago by a very famous artist. And one day somebody said — 'I'll take *him!*' — and he pointed at me. So — I had to go."

He hid his eyes for a moment behind the Dolphin's fin.

"What happened then?" demanded Jane. "How did you get to our Park?"

"In a packing-case," said Neleus calmly, and laughed at

their look of astonishment. "Oh, we always travel that way, you know. My family is very much in demand. People want us for Parks or Museums or Gardens. So they buy us and send us by Parcel Post. It never seems to occur to them that some of us might be — lonely." He choked a little on the word. Then he flung up his head with a lordly gesture. "But don't let's think about that!" he cried. "It's been much better since you two came. Oh, Jane and Michael, I know you so well — as if you were part of my family. I know about Michael's Kite and his Compass; and the Doulton Bowl, and Robertson Ay, and the things you have for supper. Didn't you ever notice me listening? And reading the fairy-tales over your shoulders?"

Jane and Michael shook their heads.

"I know *Alice in Wonderland* by heart," he went on. "And most of *Robinson Crusoe*. And *Everything a Lady Should Know,* which is Mary Poppins' favourite. But best of all are the coloured comics, especially the one called *Lot-o'-Fun.* What happened to Tiger Tim this week? Did he get away safely from Uncle Moppsy?"

"The new one comes out today," said Jane. "We'll all read it together!"

"Oh, dear! How happy I am!" cried Neleus. "The Elephant's Child, and a new *Lot-o'-Fun,* and my legs like the wings of a bird. I don't know when my Birthday is, but I think it must be today!" He hugged the Dolphin and the book in his arms and capered across the grass.

"Hi! Ting-aling-aling! Look where you're going!" the Ice Cream Man gave a warning cry. He was wheeling his barrow along by the Lake. The printed notice in front of it said:

STOP ME AND BUY ONE

WHAT WONDERFUL WEATHER!

"Stop! Stop! Stop! Stop!" cried the children wildly, as they ran towards the barrow.

"Chocolate!" said Michael.

"Lemon!" cried Jane.

And the fat little Twins put out their hands and gladly took what was given them.

"And wot about you!" said the Ice Cream Man, as Neleus came and stood shyly beside him.

"I don't know what to choose," said Neleus. "I never had one before."

"Wot! Never 'ad a Nice? Wot's the matter — weak stum-mick? A boy your size should know all about Ices! 'Ere!" The Ice Cream Man fished inside his barrow and brought out a Raspberry Bar. "Take this and see 'ow you like it!"

Neleus broke the bar with his marble fingers. He popped one half in the Dolphin's mouth and began to lick the other.

"Delicious," he said, "much better than seaweed."

"Seaweed? I should think so! Wot's seaweed got to do with it? But — talking of seaweed, that's a nice big Cod!" The Ice Cream Man waved his hand at the Dolphin. "If you took it along to the Fishmonger 'e'd give you a fancy price."

The Dolphin gave its tail a flick and its face looked very indignant.

"Oh, I don't want to sell him," said Neleus quickly. "He isn't just a fish — he's a friend!"

"A fishy kind of friend!" said the man. "Why doesn't 'e tell you to put on your clothes? You'll catch your death run-ning round stark naked. Well, no offence meant! Ting-aling! Ting-aling!" He rode away whistling and ringing his bell.

Neleus glanced at the children out of the corner of his eye and the three burst out into peals of laughter.

"Oh, dear!" cried Neleus, gasping for breath. "I believe he thinks I'm human! Shall I run and tell him he's made a mistake? That I haven't worn clothes for two thousand years and never caught even a sniffle?"

He was just about to dart after the barrow when Michael gave a shout.

"Look out! Here's Willoughby!" he cried, and swallowed the rest of his Ice in one gulp.

For Willoughby, who belonged to Miss Lark, had a habit of jumping up at the children and snatching the food from their hands. He had rough, bouncy, vulgar manners and no respect for anyone. But what else could you expect of a dog who was half an Airedale and half a Retriever and the worst half of both?

There he came, lolloping over the grass, sticking out his tongue. Andrew, who was as well-bred as Willoughby was common, tripped gracefully after him. And Miss Lark herself followed breathlessly.

"Just out for a spin before Tea!" she trilled. "Such a beau-

tiful day and the dogs insisted — Good gracious, what is that I see?"

She broke off, panting, and stared at Neleus. Her face, already red, grew redder, and she looked extremely indignant.

"You naughty, wicked boy!" she cried. "What are you doing to that poor fish? Don't you know it will die if it stays out of water?"

Neleus raised a marble eyebrow. The Dolphin swung its tail over its mouth to hide a marble smile.

"You see?" said Miss Lark. "It's writhing in agony! You must put it back into water this minute!"

"Oh, I couldn't do that," said Neleus quickly. "I'm afraid he'd be lonely without me." He was trying to be polite to Miss Lark. But the Dolphin was not. He flapped his tail and wriggled and grinned in a very discourteous manner.

"Don't answer me back! Fish are never lonely! You are just making silly excuses."

Miss Lark made an angry gesture towards the green bench.

"I do think, Mary Poppins," she said, "you might keep an eye on the children! This naughty boy, whoever he is, must put that fish back where he got it!"

Mary Poppins favoured Miss Lark with a stare. "I'm afraid that's quite impossible, ma'am. He'd have to go too far."

"Far or near — it doesn't matter. He must put it back

this instant. It's cruelty to animals and it shouldn't be allowed. Andrew and Willoughby — come with me! I shall
go at once and tell the Lord Mayor!"

Away she bustled, with the dogs at her heels. Willoughby,
as he trotted by, winked rudely at the Dolphin.

"And tell him to put his clothes on! He'll get sunburnt,
running about like that!" shrieked Miss Lark, as she hurried off.

Neleus gave a little spurt of laughter and flung himself
down on the grass.

"Sunburnt!" he choked. "Oh, Mary Poppins, does nobody guess I'm made of marble?"

"Humph!" replied Mary Poppins, snorting. And Neleus
tossed her a mischievous smile.

"That's what the Sea Lions say!" he said, "They sit on
the rocks and say 'Humph!' to the sunset!"

"Indeed?" she said tartly. And Jane and Michael waited,
trembling, for what was surely coming. But nothing happened. Her face had an answering look of mischief and the
blue eyes and the marble eyes smiled gently at each other.

"Neleus," she said quietly, "you have ten minutes more.
You can come with us to the Bookstall and back."

"And then —— ?" he said, with a questioning look, as
he tightened his arms round the Dolphin.

She did not answer. She looked across the sparkling
Lake and nodded towards the pedestal.

"Oh, can't he stay longer, Mary Poppins —— ?" the children began to protest. But the eager question froze on their lips, for Mary Poppins was glaring.

"I said ten minutes," she remarked. "And ten minutes is what I meant. You needn't look at me like that, either. I am not a Grisly Gorilla."

"Oh, don't start arguing!" cried Neleus. "We mustn't waste a second!" He sprang to his feet and seized Jane's hand. "Show me the way to the Bookstall!" he said. And drew her away through the spreading sunlight and over the grassy lawns.

Behind them Mary Poppins lifted the Twins into the perambulator and hurried along with Michael.

Lightly across the summer grasses ran Jane and the Marble Boy. His curls flew out on the wind with hers and her hot breath blew on his marble cheeks. Within her soft and living fingers the marble hand grew warmer.

"This way!" she cried, as she tugged at his arm and drew him into the Lime Walk.

At the end of it, by the Far Gate, stood the gaily painted bookstall. A bright sign nailed above it said:

MR. FOLLY

BOOKS PAPERS AND MAGAZINES

YOU WANT THEM

I'VE GOT THEM

A frill of coloured magazines hung round the Bookstall; and as the children raced up, Mr. Folly popped his head through a gap in the frill. He had a round, quiet, lazy face that looked as though nothing in the world could disturb it.

"Well, if it isn't Jane Banks and Friend!" he remarked mildly. "I think I can guess what you've come for!"

"*The Evening News* and *Lot-o'-Fun*," panted Jane, as she put down the pennies.

Neleus seized the coloured comic and skimmed the pages quickly.

"Does Tiger Tim get away?" cried Michael, as he dashed up, breathless, behind them.

"Yes, he does!" cried Neleus, with a shout of joy. "Listen! Tiger Tim Escapes Clutches of Uncle Moppsy. His New Adventure with Old Man Dogface. Watch Out For Another Tiger Tim Story Next Week!"

"Hooray!" shouted Michael, peering round the Dolphin's shoulder to get a look at the pictures.

Mr. Folly was eyeing Neleus with interest. "That's a fine young whale you got there, sonny! Seems almost 'uman. Where did you catch him?"

"I didn't," said Neleus, glancing up. "He was given to me as a present."

"Fancy that! Well, he makes a nice pet! And where do *you* come from? Where's yer Ma?"

"She's a long way from here," replied Neleus gravely.

"Too bad!" Mr. Folly wagged his head. "Dad away, too?" Neleus smiled and nodded.

"You don't say! Goodness, you must be lonely!" Mr. Folly glanced at the marble body. "And cold as well, I shouldn't wonder, with not a stitch on your bones!" He made a jingling noise in his pocket and thrust out his hand to Neleus.

"There! Get yourself something to wear with that. Can't go around with nothing on. Pneumonia, you know! And chilblains!"

Neleus stared at the silver thing in his hand.

"What is it?" he asked curiously.

"That's a 'Arf-crown," said Mr. Folly. "Don't tell me you never saw one!"

"No, I never did," said Neleus, smiling. And the Dolphin gazed at the coin with interest.

"Well, I declare! You poor little chap! Stark naked and never seen a 'Arf-crown! Someone ought to be taking care of you!" Mr. Folly glanced reproachfully at Mary Poppins. And she gave him an outraged glare.

"Someone *is* taking care of him, thank you!" she said. As she spoke she unbuttoned her new white jacket and slipped it round Neleus' shoulders.

"There!" she said gruffly. "You won't be cold now. And no thanks to *you*, Mr. Folly!"

Neleus looked from the coat to Mary Poppins and his marble eyes grew wider. "You mean — I can keep it always?" he asked.

She nodded, and looked away.

"Oh, dear sweet Sea Lion — thank you!" he cried, and he hugged her waist in his marble arms. "Look at me, Jane, in my new white coat! Look at me, Michael, in my beautiful buttons." He ran excitedly from one to the other to show off his new possession.

"That's right," said Mr. Folly, beaming. "Much better be sure than sorry! And the 'Arf-crown will buy you a nice pair of trousers —— "

"Not tonight," interrupted Mary Poppins. "We're late as it is. Now Best Foot Forward and home we go, and I'll thank you all not to dawdle."

The sun was swiftly moving westwards as she trundled the pram down the Lime Walk. The Band at the end of the Park was silent. The flowery sunshades had all gone home. The trees stood still and straight in the shadows. The Park Keeper was nowhere to be seen.

Jane and Michael walked on either side of Neleus and linked their hands through his marble arms. A silence was over the human children and over the marble child between them.

"I love you, Neleus," Jane said softly. "I wish you could stay with us always."

"I love you, too," he answered, smiling. "But I must go back. I promised."

"I suppose you couldn't leave the Dolphin?" said Michael, stroking the marble fin.

Jane looked at him angrily.

"Oh, Michael — how can you be so selfish! How would you like to spend your life, all alone up there on a pedestal?"

"I'd like it — if I could have the Dolphin, and call Mary Poppins a Sea Lion!"

"I tell you what, Michael!" said Neleus quickly. "You can't have the Dolphin — he's part of me. But the Half-crown isn't. I'll give you that." He pushed the money into Michael's hand. "And Jane must have the book," he went on. "But promise, Jane, and cross your heart, that you'll let me read it over your shoulder. And every week you must come to the bench and read me the new *Lot-o'-Fun*."

He gave the book a last long look and tucked it under her arm.

"Oh, I promise, Neleus!" she said faithfully, and crossed her heart with her hand.

"I'll be waiting for you," said Neleus softly. "I'll never, never forget."

"Walk up and don't chatter!" hissed Mary Poppins, as she turned towards the Lake.

The perambulator creaked and groaned as it trundled on its way. But high above the creak of the wheels they could hear a well-known voice. They tiptoed up behind Mary Poppins as she walked to the shadowy water.

"I never done it!" the voice protested. "And wouldn't — not if you paid me!"

At the edge of the Lake, by the empty pedestal, stood

the Lord Mayor with two Aldermen. And before them,
waving his arms and shouting, and generally behaving in a
peculiar manner, was the Park Keeper.

"It's none of my doing, Your Honour!" he pleaded. "I
can look you straight in the eye!"

"Nonsense, Smith!" said the Lord Mayor sternly. "You
are the person responsible for the Park statues. And only
you could have done it!"

"You might as well confess!" advised the First Alderman.

"It won't save you, of course," the Second added, "but
you'll *feel* so much better!"

"But I didn't *do* it, I'm telling you!" The Park Keeper
clasped his hands in a frenzy.

"Stop quibbling, Smith. You're wasting my time!" The
Lord Mayor shook his head impatiently. "First, I have to
go looking for a naked boy who I hear is maltreating some
wretched fish. A salmon, Miss Lark said — or was it a
halibut? And now, as if this wasn't enough, I find the most
valuable of our statues is missing from its pedestal. I am
shocked and disgusted. I trusted you, Smith. And look
how you repay me!"

"I *am* looking. I mean, I don't *have* to look! Oh, I don't
know what I'm saying, Your Grace! But I *do* know I never
touched that statchew!"

The Keeper glanced round wildly for help and his eye
fell on Mary Poppins. He gave a cry of horrified triumph
and flung out his hand accusingly.

"Your Worship, *there's* the guilty party! She done it or I'll eat me 'At!"

The Lord Mayor glanced at Mary Poppins and back to the Park Keeper.

"I'm ashamed of you, Smith!" he shook his head sorrowfully. "Putting the blame on a perfectly respectable, innocent young woman taking her charges for an afternoon airing! How could you?"

He bowed courteously to Mary Poppins, who returned the bow with a lady-like smile.

"Innocent! *'Er!*" the Park Keeper screamed. "You don't know what you're sayin', my Lord! As soon as that girl comes into the Park, the place begins to go crosswise. Merry-go-rounds jumpin' up in the sky, people coming down on kites and rockets, the Prime Minister bobbing round on balloons — and it's all *your* doing — you Caliban!" He shook his fist wildly at Mary Poppins.

"Poor fellow! Poor fellow! His mind is unhinged!" said the First Alderman sadly.

"Perhaps we'd better get some handcuffs," the Second whispered nervously.

"Do what you like with me! 'Ang me, why don't yer? But it wasn't me wot done it!" Overcome with misery, the Park Keeper flung himself against the pedestal and sobbed bitterly.

Mary Poppins turned and beckoned to Neleus. He ran to her side on marble feet and leaned his head gently against her.

The Park Keeper flung himself against the pedestal

"Is it time?" he whispered, glancing up.

She nodded quickly. Then bending she took him in her arms and kissed his marble brow. For a moment Neleus clung to her as though he could never let her go. Then he broke away, smothering a sob.

"Good-bye, Jane and Michael. Don't forget me!" He pressed his chilly cheek to theirs. And before they could even say a word he had darted away among the shadows and was running towards his pedestal.

"I never 'ad no luck!" wailed the Keeper. "Never since I was a boy!"

"And you won't have any now, my man, unless you put back that statue." The Lord Mayor fixed him with an angry eye.

But Jane and Michael were looking neither at the Park Keeper nor the Lord Mayor. They were watching a curly head appear at the far side of the pedestal.

Up scrambled Neleus, over the ledge, dragging the Dolphin after him. His marble body blazed white and bright in a fading shaft of sunlight. Then with a gesture, half-gay, half-sad, he put up a little marble hand and waved them all farewell. As they waved back he seemed to tremble, but that may have been the tears in their eyes. They watched him draw the Dolphin to him, so close that its marble melted to his. Then he smoothed his curls with a marble hand and bent his head and was still. Even Mary Poppins' pink-and-white jacket seemed turned to lifeless marble.

"I can't put it back if I never took it!" the Park Keeper went on sobbing and shouting.

"Now, see here, Smith——" the Lord Mayor began. Then he gave a gasp and staggered sideways with his hand clasped to his brow. "My Jumping Giraffes! It's come back——" he cried. "And there's something different about it!"

He peered more closely at the statue and burst into roars of delighted laughter. He took off his hat and waved it wildly and slapped the Park Keeper on the back.

"Smith—you rogue! So *that* was your secret! Why didn't you tell us at first, my man? It certainly is a splendid surprise! Well, you needn't go on pretending now——"

For the Park Keeper, speechless with amazement, was goggling up at Neleus.

"Gentlemen!" The Lord Mayor turned to the Aldermen. "We have sadly misjudged this poor fellow. He has proved himself not only an excellent servant of the community—but an artist as well. Do you see what he has done to the statue? He has added a little marble coat with collar and cuffs of pink. A *great* improvement, to my mind, Smith! I *never* approved of naked statues."

"Nor I!" the First Alderman shook his head.

"Certainly not!" said the Second.

"Never fear, my dear Smith. You shall have your reward. From today your wages will be raised one shilling and an extra stripe will be sewn on your sleeve. Furthermore, I shall speak of you to His Majesty when I make my next report."

And the Lord Mayor, with another ceremonious bow to Mary Poppins, swept majestically away, humbly followed by the two Aldermen.

The Park Keeper, looking as though he were not sure if he were on his head or his heels, stared after them. Then he turned his popping eyes to the statue and stared again at that. The Marble Boy and his marble fish gazed thoughtfully down at the Lake. They were as still and quiet and silent as they had always been.

"Now home again, home again, jiggety-jog!" Mary Poppins raised a beckoning finger and the children followed without a word. The Half-crown lay in Michael's palm, burning and bright and solid. And cold as the marble hand of Neleus was the book beneath Jane's arm.

Along the Walk they marched in silence thinking their secret thoughts. And presently, on the grass behind them, there came the thud of feet. They turned to find the Park Keeper running heavily towards them. He had taken off his coat and was waving it, like a blue-and-red flag, at the end of his walking stick. He pulled up, panting, beside the perambulator and held out the coat to Mary Poppins.

"Take it!" he said breathlessly. "I just been looking at that Boy back there. He's wearin' yours — with the four pink buttons. And you'll need one when it gets chilly."

Mary Poppins calmly took the coat and slipped it over her shoulders. Her own reflection smiled conceitedly at her from the polished brass buttons.

"Thank you," she said primly, to the Park Keeper.

He stood before her in his shirt-sleeves, shaking his head like a puzzled dog.

"I suppose *you* understand what it all means?" he said wistfully.

"I suppose I do," she replied smugly.

And without another word, she gave the perambulator a little push and sent it bowling past him. He was still staring after her, scratching his head, as she passed through the gate of the Park.

Mr. Banks, on his way home from the Office, whistled to them as they crossed the Lane.

"Well, Mary Poppins!" he greeted her. "You're very smart in your blue-and-red jacket! Have you joined the Salvation Army?"

"No, sir," she replied, primly. And the look she gave him made it quite clear she had no intention of explaining.

"It's the Park Keeper's coat," Jane told him hurriedly.

"He gave it to her just now," added Michael.

"What — Smith? He gave her the jacket of his uniform? Whatever for?" exclaimed Mr. Banks.

But Jane and Michael were suddenly silent. They could feel Mary Poppins' gimlet eyes making holes in the backs of their heads. They dared not go on with the story.

"Well, never mind!" said Mr. Banks calmly. "I suppose she did something to deserve it!"

They nodded. But they knew he would never know what she had done, not even if he lived to be fifty. They walked up the garden path beside him, clasping the coin and the book.

And as they went they thought of the child who had given them those gifts, the Marble Boy who for one short hour had danced and played in the Park. They thought of him standing alone on his pedestal, with his arm flung lovingly round his Dolphin — forever silent, forever still and the sweet light gone from his face. Darkness would come down upon him and the stars and the night would wrap him round. Proud and lonely he would stand there, looking down upon the waters of the little Lake, dreaming of the great sea and his home so far away....

CHAPTER FIVE

Peppermint Horses

i!" shouted Mr. Banks, angrily, as he rattled the umbrellas in the Elephant's Leg that stood in the front hall.

"What is it now, George?" called Mrs. Banks, from the foot of the kitchen stairs.

"Somebody's taken my walking sticks!" Mr. Banks sounded like a wounded tiger.

"Here they are, Sir!" said Mary Poppins, as she tripped down from the Nursery. In one hand she carried a silver-headed ebony cane. From the other swung a grey ash stick with a curved nobbly handle. Without another word, and looking very superior, she handed the sticks to Mr. Banks.

"Oh!" he said, rather taken aback. "Why did you want them, Mary Poppins? I hope you haven't got a bad leg!"

"No, thank you, Sir!" she said with a sniff. And you knew by the haughty tone of her voice that Mr. Banks had insulted her. A bad leg, indeed! As if her legs, as well as every other part of her, were not in perfect condition!

"It was us!" said Jane and Michael together, peering out at their Father from behind Mary Poppins.

"You! What's the matter with *your* fat legs? Are they lame, or crippled or what?"

"Nothing's the matter," said Michael plaintively. "We wanted the sticks for horses."

"What! My Great-uncle Herbert's ebony cane and the stick I won in the Church Bazaar!" Mr. Banks could hardly believe his ears.

"Well, we've nothing to ride on!" grumbled Jane.

"Why not the rocking-horse — dear old Dobbin?" called Mrs. Banks from the kitchen.

"I hate old Dobbin. He creaks!" said Michael, and he stamped his foot at his Mother.

"But Dobbin doesn't *go* anywhere. We want real horses!" protested Jane.

"And I'm to provide them, I suppose!" Mr. Banks strode, fuming, down the hall. "Three meals a day are not enough! Warm clothes and shoes are merely trifles! Now you want horses! Horses, indeed! Are you sure you wouldn't prefer a camel?"

Michael looked at his Father with a pained expression. Really, he thought, what shocking behaviour! But aloud he said patiently ——

"No, thank you. Just horses!"

"Well, you'll get them when the moon turns blue! That's all I can say!" snapped Mr. Banks.

"How often does that happen?" Jane enquired.

Mr. Banks looked at her angrily. What stupid children I've got, he thought. Can't understand a figure of speech!

"Oh — every thousand years or so. Once in a life-time — if you're lucky!" he said crossly. And, stuffing the cane into the Elephant's Leg, he hooked the ash stick over his arm and started for the City.

Mary Poppins smiled as she watched him go. A curious, secret smile it was, and the children wondered what it meant.

Mrs. Banks came bustling up the kitchen stairs. "Oh dear! Mary Poppins, what do you think! Miss Lark's dog Willoughby has just been in and eaten a tyre off the perambulator!"

"Yes, ma'am," replied Mary Poppins calmly, as though nothing that Willoughby ever did could possibly surprise her.

"But what shall we do about the shopping?" Mrs. Banks was almost in tears.

"I really couldn't say, I'm sure." Mary Poppins gave her head a toss, as though neither dogs nor perambulators were any concern of hers.

"Oh, must we go shopping?" grumbled Jane.

"I'm sick of walking," said Michael crossly. "I'm sure it's bad for my health."

Mrs. Banks took no notice of them. "Perhaps, Mary Poppins," she suggested nervously, "you could leave

Annabel at home today and take Robertson Ay to carry the parcels."

"He's asleep in the wheelbarrow," Jane informed them. She had looked through the window, just after breakfast, and seen him taking his morning rest.

"Well, he won't be there long," said Mary Poppins. And she stalked out into the garden.

She was quite right. He wasn't there long. She must have said something Really Awful, for as they trailed after her down the path Robertson Ay was waiting at the garden gate.

"Keep up and don't straggle, if you please! This is not a Tortoise Parade." Mary Poppins took a Twin by each hand and hurried them along beside her.

"Day in and day out, it's always the same. I never get a moment's peace." Robertson Ay gave a stifled yawn as he handed Jane his hat to carry and stumbled along beside her.

Down the High Street marched Mary Poppins, glancing at the windows now and again to admire her own reflection.

Her first stop was at Mr. Trimlet's — Ironmonger, Hardware and Garden Tools.

"One mouse-trap!" she said haughtily, as she darted in at the door of the shop and read from Mrs. Banks' list.

Mr. Trimlet was a bony man with a large purplish face. He was sitting behind the counter with his hat on the back of his head. And the morning paper was propped around him like an old Chinese screen.

"Only one?" he asked rudely, peering round the edge of the screen to look at Mary Poppins. "Sorry, Miss!" he said with a leer. "But one trap wouldn't be worth me while!" He shook his head and was about to turn away when he caught the look on her face. His purple cheeks turned the colour of lilac.

"Just my joke," he said hurriedly. "No offence meant! Why, I'd sell 'alf a mouse-trap if I thought *you* wanted it. Not to mention a nice bit o' cheese to go with it."

"One mincing machine," said Mary Poppins, as she fixed him with a stare.

"And I'll throw in a pound of steak for luck," said Mr. Trimlet eagerly.

Mary Poppins took no notice.

"Half-a-dozen pot cleaners, one tin of bees' wax, one floor mop," she read out quickly.

"Setting up 'ouse?" enquired Mr. Trimlet, smiling nervously as he tied up the parcels.

"A packet of nails and a garden rake," she went on. She looked right through his purple face as though it were made of glass.

"And wot about the sawdust?" he enquired. "All that wot them children has spilt?"

Mary Poppins spun round. Jane and Michael and the Twins were sitting comfortably on a fat brown sack, and their weight had squeezed a stream of sawdust out on to the floor. Her eyes blazed.

"If you don't get up this minute ——" she began. And her voice was so frightful that they sprang to their feet without waiting to hear the rest of the sentence. Robertson Ay, who had been asleep on a garden-roller, woke up with a start and began to collect the parcels.

"We were only resting our legs ——" Michael began.

"One More Word and you'll find yourself resting in Bed! I warn you!" she told him fiercely.

"I'll make no charge," declared Mr. Trimlet, as he hurriedly swept up the sawdust. "Seein' it's you!" he added eagerly, still trying to be friendly.

Mary Poppins gave him a contemptuous stare.

"There's paint on your nose," she announced calmly, and stalked out of the shop.

Then off she went, like a human whirlwind, speeding up the High Street. And off went the children and Robertson Ay, wheeling behind her like the tail of a comet.

At the Baker's she bought a loaf of bread, two boxes of tarts and some ginger biscuits.

"Don't mind me," sighed Robertson Ay as she piled them into his arms.

"I won't!" she retorted cheerfully, as she hurried on to the Greengrocer's for peas, beans and cherries.

"The Last Straw breaks the Camel's back," said Robertson Ay, as she thrust them at him.

"So they say!" she remarked with a chilly smile and consulted her list again.

The next place was the Stationer's, where she bought a bottle of ink; and then she went to the Chemist for a packet of mustard plasters.

By now they had come to the end of the High Street. But still Mary Poppins did not stop. The children looked at each other and sighed. There were no more shops. Where could she be going?

"Oh, dear, Mary Poppins, my legs are breaking!" said Michael, limping pathetically.

"Can't we go home now, Mary Poppins? My shoes are worn out!" complained Jane.

And the Twins began to whimper and whine like a couple of fretful puppies.

Mary Poppins regarded them all with disgust.

"A set of Jellyfish — that's what you are! You haven't a backbone between you!"

And popping the shopping-list into her bag, she gave a quick contemptuous sniff and hurried round the corner.

"A Jellyfish swims," said Michael angrily. "And it doesn't have to go shopping!" He was so tired that he almost didn't care whether Mary Poppins heard him or not.

The breeze blew gently from the Park, full of the scents of the morning. It smelt of laurel leaves and moss, and something else that was vaguely familiar. What could it be? Jane sniffed the air.

"Michael!" she whispered. "I smell Peppermint!"

Michael sniffed like a sulky little dog.

"Um-hum," he admitted, "I do, too!"

And then it was that they both noticed the red-and-green umbrella. It stood beside the iron railings on the Town side of the Park. Against it leaned a large white signboard.

MISS CALICO

CONFECTIONER

HORSES FOR HIRE

said the words in big black letters.

The children stared.

For beneath the red-and-green umbrella sat one of the strangest little figures they had ever seen. At first they could not make out what it was, for it sparkled and glittered like a diamond. Then they saw that it was a small elderly lady with a skinny, leathery, yellow face and a mane of short white hair. The glitter and sparkle came from her dress, which was covered from collar to hem with pins. They stuck out all over her, like the quills of a hedgehog, and whenever she moved they flashed in the sunlight. In her hand she held a riding-whip. And every now and again she cracked it at one of the passers-by.

"Peppermint Candy! Bargain Prices! All of it made of Finest Sugar!" she cried in a little whinnying voice as the whip swished through the air.

"Come on, Michael!" said Jane excitedly, forgetting how tired she was.

He took her hand and let her drag him towards the striped umbrella. And as they drew nearer the sparkling figure, they saw a sight that filled them with hunger. For beside her stood a pottery jar that was filled with pepper-mint walking-sticks.

> "Sugar and Spice
> And all that's nice

At a Very Special
Bargain Price!"

sang the little old lady, cracking her whip.

And just at that moment she turned her head and spied the straggling group. Her dark eyes glittered like little black currants as she thrust out a bird-like hand.

"Well, I never! If it isn't Mary Poppins! I haven't seen you in a month of Tuesdays!"

"The same to you, so to speak, Miss Calico!" Mary Poppins replied politely.

"Well, it all just goes to show!" said Miss Calico. "If you know what I mean!" she added, grinning. Then her bright black gaze fell upon the children.

"Why, Mercy Me and a Jumping Bean! What a quartet of sulky faces! Cross-patch, draw the latch! You all look as if you'd lost something!"

"Their tempers," said Mary Poppins grimly.

Miss Calico's eyebrows went up with a rush, and her pins began to flash.

"Thundering Tadpoles! Think of that! Well, what's lost must be found — that's the law! Now — where did you lose 'em?"

The little black eyes went from one to another and somehow they all felt guilty.

"I think it must have been in the High Street," said Jane in a stifled whisper.

"Tut! Tut! All that way back? And *why* did you lose 'em, might one ask?"

Michael shuffled his feet and his face grew red. "We didn't want to go on walking——" he began shamefacedly. But the sentence was never finished. Miss Calico interrupted him with a loud shrill cackle.

"Who does? Who does? I'd like to know? Nobody wants to go on walking. I wouldn't do it myself if you paid me. Not for a sackful of rubies!"

Michael stared. Could it really be true? Had he found at last a grown-up person who felt as he did about walking?

"Why, I haven't walked for centuries," said Miss Calico. "And what's more, none of my family does. What — stump on the ground on two flat feet? They'd think that quite beneath them!" She cracked her whip and her pins flashed brightly as she shook her finger at the children.

"Take my advice and always ride. Walking will only make you grow. And where does it get you? Pretty near nowhere! Ride, I say! Ride — and see the world!"

"But we've nothing to ride on!" Jane protested, looking round to see what Miss Calico rode. For, in spite of the notice "Horses for Hire" there wasn't even a donkey in sight.

"Nothing to ride on? Snakes alive! That's a very unfortunate state of affairs!"

Miss Calico's voice had a mournful sound but her black eyes twinkled impishly as she glanced at Mary Poppins.

She gave a little questioning nod and Mary Poppins nodded back.

"Well, it might have been worse!" cried Miss Calico, as she whipped up a handful of sticks. "If you can't have horses — what about these? *At* least they'll help you along a bit. I can let you have 'em for a pin apiece."

The scent of peppermint filled the air, The four lost tempers came creeping back as they searched their clothes for pins. They wriggled and giggled, and peeked and pried, but never a pin could they find.

"Oh, what shall we do, Mary Poppins?" cried Jane. "We haven't a pin between us!"

"I should hope not!" she replied, with a snort. "The children *I* care for are properly mended."

She gave a little disgusted sniff. Then turning back the lapel of her coat, she handed a pin to each of the children. Robertson Ay, who was dozing against the railings, woke up with a start as she handed him another.

"Stick 'em in!" shrieked Miss Calico, leaning towards them. "Don't mind if they prick. I'm too tough to feel 'em!"

They pushed their pins in among the others and her dress seemed to shine more brightly than ever as she handed out the sticks.

Laughing and shouting, they seized and waved them and the scent of peppermint grew stronger.

"I shan't mind walking now!" cried Michael, as he nibbled the end of his stick. A shrill little cry broke on the air, like a faint protesting neigh. But Michael was sampling the Peppermint Candy and was far too absorbed to hear it.

"I'm not going to eat mine," Jane said quickly. "I'm going to keep it always."

Miss Calico glanced at Mary Poppins and a curious look was exchanged between them.

"If you can!" said Miss Calico, cackling loudly. "You may keep 'em *all*, if you can — and welcome! Stick 'em in firmly, don't mind me!" She handed a stick to Robertson Ay as he stuck his pin in her sleeve.

"And now," said Mary Poppins politely, "if you'll excuse us, Miss Calico, we'll get along home to dinner!"

"Oh, wait, Mary Poppins!" protested Michael. "We haven't bought a stick for you!" An awful thought had come to him. What if she hadn't another pin? Would he have to share his stick with her?

"Humph!" she said, with a toss of her head. "*I'm* not afraid of breaking my legs, like some people I could mention!"

"Tee-hee! Ha-ha! Excuse me laughing! As if *she* needed a walking stick!"

Miss Calico gave a bird-like chirp, as though Michael had said something funny.

"Well, pleased to have met you!" said Mary Poppins, as she shook Miss Calico's hand.

"The Pleasure is mine, I assure you, Miss Poppins!
Now, remember my warning! Always ride! Good-bye,
good-bye!" Miss Calico trilled. She seemed to have quite
forgotten the fact that none of them had any horses.

"Peppermint Candy! Bargain Prices! All of it made of
the Finest Sugar!" they heard her shouting as they turned
away.

"Got a Pin?" she enquired of a passer-by, a well-dressed
gentleman wearing an eye-glass. He carried a brief-case
under his arm. It was marked in gold letters

LORD CHANCELLOR

DISPATCHES

"Pin?" said the gentleman. "Certainly not! Where
would *I* get such a thing as a Pin?"

"Nothing for nothing, that's the law! You can't get a
stick if you've got no pin!"

"Take one o' mine, duck! I got plenty!" said a large fat
woman who was tramping past. She hitched a basket under her arm and, plucking a handful of pins from her shawl,
she offered them to the Lord Chancellor.

"One Pin Only! Bargain Prices! Never Pay Two when
you're asked for One!" Miss Calico cried in her hen-like
cackle. She gave the Lord Chancellor a stick and he hooked
it over his arm and went on.

"You and your laws!" said the fat woman laughing, as she stuck a pin in Miss Calico's skirt. "Well, gimme a strong one, ducky, do! I'm hardly a Fairy Fay!" Miss Calico gave her a long, thick stick and she grasped the handle in her hand and leaned her weight against it.

"Feed the birds! Tuppence a bag! Thank you, my dear!" cried the fat woman gaily.

"Michael!" cried Jane, with a gasp of surprise, "I do believe it's the Bird Woman!"

But before he had a chance to reply, a very strange thing happened. As the fat woman leaned her weight on the stick it gave a little upward swing. Then, swooping under her spreading skirts, it heaved her into the air.

"Ups a daisy! 'Ere I go!" The Bird Woman seized the peppermint handle and wildly clutched her basket.

Off swept the walking stick over the pavement and up across the railings. A long, loud neighing filled the air and the children stared in amazement.

"Hold tightly!" Michael shouted anxiously.

" 'Old tight yourself!" the Bird Woman answered, for his stick was already leaping beneath him.

"Hi, Jane! Mine's doing it, too!" he shrieked, as the stick bore him swiftly away.

"Be careful, Michael!" Jane called after him. But just at that moment her own stick wobbled and made a long plunge upwards. Away it swooped on the trail of Michael's, with Jane astride its pink-and-white back. Over the laurel hedge she rode and as she cleared the lilac bushes a crackling shape sped past her. It was Robertson Ay with his arms full of parcels. He was lying lengthways along his stick and dozing as he rode.

"I'll race you to the oak tree, Jane!" cried Michael, as she trotted up.

"Quietly, please! No horseplay, Michael! Put your hats straight and follow me!"

Mary Poppins, on her parrot umbrella, rode past them at a canter. Neatly and primly, as though she were in a rocking chair, she sat on the black silk folds. In her hand she held two leading strings attached to the Twins' pink sticks.

"All of 'em made of the Finest Sugar!" Miss Calico's voice came floating up as the earth fell away beneath them.

"She's selling hundreds of sticks!" cried Michael. For the sky was quickly filling with riders.

"There goes Aunt Flossie — over the dahlias!" cried Jane, as she pointed downwards. Below them rode a middle-aged lady. Her feather boa streamed out on the wind and her hat was blowing sideways.

"So it is!" said Michael, staring with interest. "And there's Miss Lark — with the dogs!"

Above the weeping-willow trees a neat little peppermint stick came trotting. On its back sat Miss Lark, looking rather nervous, and behind her rode the dogs. Willoughby, looking none the worse for the perambulator tyre, smiled rudely at the children. But Andrew kept his eyes tight shut as heights always made him giddy.

Ka-lop! Ka-lop! Ka-lop! Ka-lop! came the sound of galloping hooves.

"Help! Help! Murder! Earthquakes!" cried a hoarse, distracted voice.

The children turned to see Mr. Trimlet riding madly up behind them. His hands clung tightly to the Peppermint Candy and his face had turned quite white.

"I tried to eat my stick," he wailed, "and look what it did to me!"

"Bargain Prices! Only one Pin! You get what you give!" came Miss Calico's voice.

By this time the sky was like a race-course. The riders came from all directions; and it seemed to the children that everyone they knew had bought a peppermint horse. A man in a feathered hat rode by and they recognised him as one of the Aldermen. In the distance they caught a glimpse of the Matchman, as he trotted along on a bright pink stick. The Sweep raced past with his sooty brushes and the Ice Cream Man cantered up beside him, licking a Strawberry Bar.

"Out of the way! Make room! Make room!" cried a loud, important voice.

And they saw the Lord Chancellor dashing along at break-neck speed. He leaned low over the neck of his stick as though he were riding a Derby Winner. His eye-glass was firmly stuck in his eye and his briefcase bounced up and down as he rode.

"Important Dispatches!" they heard him shout. "I must get to the Palace in time for Lunch! Make room! Make room!" And away he galloped and soon was out of sight.

What a commotion there was in the Park! Everyone jostled everyone else. "Get up!" and "Whoa there!" the riders yelled. And the walking sticks snorted like angry horses.

"Keep to the Left! No overtaking!" the Park Keeper cried, as he cantered among them.

"No Parking!" he bawled. "Pedestrians Crossing! Speed Limit Twenty Miles an Hour!"

"Feed the Birds! Tuppence a Bag!" The Bird Woman

"Out of the way! Make room! Make room!"

trotted among the crowd. She moved through a tossing surge of wings — pigeons and starlings, blackbirds and sparrows. "Feed the Birds! Tuppence a Bag!" she cried as she tossed her nuts in the air.

The Park Keeper pulled up his stick and shouted.

"Why, Mother, wot are *you* doin' 'ere? You ought to be down at St. Paul's!"

" 'Ullo, Fred, my boy! I'm feedin' the Birds! See you at Tea-time! Tuppence a Bag!"

The Park Keeper stared as she rode away.

"I never saw 'er do that before, not even when I was a boy! 'Ere! Whoa, there! Look where you're goin'!" he cried, as a bright pink walking stick streaked by.

On it rode Ellen and the Policeman who were off for their Afternoon Out.

"Oh! Oh!" shrieked Ellen. "I daren't look down! It makes me feel quite giddy!"

"Well, don't, then. Look at me instead!" said the Policeman, holding her round the waist as their stick galloped swiftly away.

On and on went the peppermint walking sticks and their pinkness shone in the morning sun. Over the trees they bore their riders, over the houses, over the clouds.

Down below them Miss Calico's voice grew fainter every moment.

"Peppermint Candy! Bargain Prices! All of them made of the Finest Sugar!"

And at last it seemed to Jane and Michael that the voice was no longer Miss Calico's, but the faint shrill neigh of a little horse in a very distant meadow.

They threaded their way through the crowding riders, bouncing upon their peppermint sticks. The wind ran swiftly by their faces and the echo of hooves was in their ears. Oh, where were they riding? Home to dinner? Or out to the uttermost ends of the earth?

And ever before them, showing the way, went the figure of Mary Poppins. She sat her umbrella with elegant ease, her hands well down on its parrot head. The pigeon's wing flew at a perfect angle, not a fold of her dress was out of place. What she was thinking, they could not tell. But her mouth had a small self-satisfied smile as though she were thoroughly pleased with herself.

Cherry-Tree Lane grew nearer and nearer. The Admiral's telescope shone in the sun.

"Oh, I wish we need never go down!" cried Michael.

"I wish we could ride all day!" cried Jane.

"I wish to be home by One O'clock. Keep up with me, please!" said Mary Poppins. She pointed the beak of her parrot umbrella towards Number Seventeen.

They sighed, though they knew it was no good sighing. They patted the necks of their walking sticks and followed her downwards through the sky.

The garden lawn, like a bright green paddock, rose slowly up to meet them. Down to it raced the peppermint sticks, rearing and prancing like polo ponies. Robertson Ay was the first to land. His stick pulled up in the pansy bed and Robertson opened his eyes and blinked. He yawned and gathered his parcels together and staggered into the house.

Down past the Cherry-Trees trotted the children. Down, down, till the grasses grazed their feet, and the sticks stood still on the lawn.

At the same moment, the parrot-headed umbrella, its black silk folds like a pair of wings, swooped down among the flowers. Mary Poppins alighted with a ladylike jump. Then she gave the umbrella a little shake and tucked it under her arm. To look at that neat, respectable pair, you would never have guessed they had crossed the Park in such a curious fashion.

"Oh, what a glorious ride!" cried Michael. "How lucky you had those pins, Mary Poppins!" He rushed to her across the lawn and hugged her round the waist.

"Is this a garden or a Jumble Sale? I'll thank you to let me go!" she snapped.

"I'll never lose my temper again! I feel so sweet and good!" said Jane.

Mary Poppins smiled disbelievingly. "How very unusual!" she remarked, as she stooped to pick up the sticks.

"I'll take mine, Mary Poppins!" said Michael, as he made a grab at a sugary handle.

But she swung the walking sticks over her head and stalked away into the house.

"I won't eat it, Mary Poppins!" he pleaded. "I shan't even nibble the handle!"

Mary Poppins took not the slightest notice. Without a word she sailed upstairs with the walking sticks under her arm.

"But they're ours!" complained Michael, turning to Jane. "Miss Calico told us to keep them!"

"No, she didn't," said Jane, with a shake of her head. "She said we might keep them if we could."

"Well, of course we can!" said Michael stoutly. "We'll keep them to ride on always!"

And indeed, the sight of the walking sticks, as they stood in a corner by Mary Poppins' bed, was very reassuring. For who, the children fondly thought, would want to steal four sticky poles of sugar? Already the pink-and-white-striped sticks seemed part of the nursery furniture.

They leaned together with handles locked, like four faithful friends. Not a movement came from any of them. They were just like any other sticks, quietly waiting in a dusty corner to go for a walk with their owners. . . .

The afternoon passed and bed-time came and the scent of peppermint filled the Nursery. Michael sniffed as he hurried in from his bath.

"They're all right!" he whispered, as Jane came in. "But I think we should stay awake tonight and see that nothing happens."

Jane nodded. She had seen those sticks do curious things and she felt that Michael was right.

So, long after Mary Poppins had gone, they lay awake and stared at the corner. The four dim shapes stood still and silent beside the neat camp bed.

"Where shall we go tomorrow?" asked Michael. "I think I'll ride over to see Aunt Flossie and ask her how she liked it." He gave a yawn and shut his right eye. He could see just as well with one, he thought. And the other could take a rest.

"I'd like to see Timbuctoo," said Jane. "It has such a beautiful sound."

There was a long pause.

"Don't you think that's a good idea, Michael?"

But Michael did not answer. He had closed the other eye — just for a moment. And in that moment he had fallen asleep.

Jane sat up, faithfully watching the sticks. She watched and watched and watched and watched, till her head fell sideways upon the pillow.

"Timbuctoo," she murmured drowsily, with her eyes on the slender shapes in the corner. And after that she said nothing more because she was much too sleepy. . . .

Downstairs the Grandfather Clock struck ten. But Jane did not hear it. She did not hear Mary Poppins creep in and undress beneath her cotton nightgown. She did not hear Mr. Banks locking the doors, nor the house as it settled down for the night. She was dreaming a beautiful dream of horses and through it came Michael calling her name.

"Jane! Jane! Jane!" came the urgent whisper.

She sprang up and tossed the hair from her eyes. Beyond Mary Poppins' sleeping shape she could see Michael sitting on the edge of his bed with his finger to his lips.

"I heard a funny noise!" he hissed.

Jane listened. Yes! She heard it, too. She held her breath as she caught the sound of a high, shrill, faraway whistle.

"Whew — ee! Whew — ee!"

It came nearer and nearer. Then, suddenly, from the night outside, they heard a shrill voice calling.

"Come, Sugar! Come, Lightfoot! Come, Candy! Come, Mint! Don't wait or you'll be late. That's the law!"

And at the same moment there was a quick scuffle in the corner by Mary Poppins' bed.

Rattle! Clash! Bang! Swoop!

And the four walking sticks, one after another, rose up and leapt out of the window.

In a flash the children were out of bed and leaning across the sill. All was darkness. The night had not a single star.

But over the Cherry-Trees something shone with a queer unearthly brilliance.

It was Miss Calico. She flashed like a little silver hedge-hog, as she rode through the sky on a peppermint stick. Her whip made little cracks in the air and her whistle pierced the still, dark night.

"Come up, you slow-coaches!" she screamed, as the four sticks followed her, neighing wildly.

"Dancer, you donkey, come up!" she called. And from somewhere, down by the kitchen steps, another stick came trotting.

"That must be Robertson Ay's!" said Jane.

"Where are you, Trixie? Come up, my girl!" Miss Calico cracked her whip again. And out from Miss Lark's best bedroom window another stick leapt to join the throng.

"Come, Stripe! Come Lollipop! Dapple and Trot!" From every direction the sticks came racing.

"Shake a leg, Blossom! Look sharp, there, Honey! Those who roam, must come home. That's the law!" She whistled them up and cracked her whip and laughed as they leapt through the air towards her.

The whole sky now was studded with sticks. It rang with the thunder of galloping hooves and the trumpeting neighs of peppermint horses. At first they looked like small black shadows with the colour gone from their shining backs. But a glow of moonrise came from the Park and soon they appeared in all their brightness. They shone and shimmered as they galloped; their pink legs flashed in the rising light.

"Come up, my fillies! Come up, my nags! All of you made of the Finest Sugar!"

High and sweet came Miss Calico's voice, as she called her horses home. Crack! went her whip as they trotted behind her, snorting and tossing their peppermint heads.

Then the moon rose, full and round and clear, above the trees of the Park. And Jane, as she saw it, gave a gasp and clutched her brother's hand.

"Oh, Michael! Look! It's blue!" she cried.

And blue indeed it was.

Out from the other side of earth the great blue moon came marching. Over the Park and over the Lane it spread its bright blue rays. It hung from the topmost peak of the sky, and shone like a lamp on the sleeping world.

And across its light, like a flock of bats, rode Miss Calico and her string of horses. Their shapes sped past the big blue moon and flashed for a moment in its brightness. Then away went the racing peppermint sticks, through the distant shining sky. The crack of the whip grew smaller and smaller. Miss Calico's voice grew far and faint. Till at last it seemed as though she and her horses had faded into the moonlight.

"All of them made of the Finest Sugar!"

A last small echo came floating back.

The children leaned on the window-sill and were silent for a moment.

Then Michael spoke.

"We couldn't keep them, after all," he said in a mournful whisper.

"She never meant us to," said Jane, as she gazed at the empty sky.

They turned together from the window, and the moon's blue light streamed into the room. It lay like water upon the floor. It crept across the children's cots till it reached the bed in the corner. Then, full and clear and bold and blue, it shone upon Mary Poppins. She did not wake. But she smiled a secret, satisfied smile as though, even in her deepest dreams, she was thoroughly pleased with herself.

They stood beside her, hardly breathing, as they watched that curious smile. Then they looked at each other and nodded wisely.

"She knows," said Michael, in a whisper. And Jane breathed an answering "Yes."

For a moment they smiled at her sleeping figure. Then they tip-toed back to their beds.

The blue moonlight lay over their pillows. It lapped them round as they closed their eyes. It gleamed upon Mary Poppins' nose as she lay in her old camp bed. And presently, as though blue moons were nothing to her, she turned her face away. She pulled the sheet up over her head and huddled down deeper under the blankets. And soon the only sound in the Nursery was Mary Poppins' snoring.

CHAPTER SIX

High Tide

nd be sure you don't drop it!" said Mary Poppins, as she handed Michael a large black bottle.

He met the warning glint in her eye and shook his head earnestly.

"I'll be extra specially careful," he promised. He could not have gone more cautiously if he had been a Burglar.

He and Jane and Mary Poppins had been on a visit to Admiral Boom to borrow a Bottle of Port for Mr. Banks. Now it was lying in Michael's arms and he was walking gingerly — pit-pat, pit-pat — like a cat on hot bricks. And dawdling along behind came Jane, holding the Spotted Cowrie Shell that Mrs. Boom had given her.

They had had a wonderful afternoon. The Admiral had sung "I Saw Three Ships a-Sailing" and shown them his full-rigged Ship in a Bottle. Mrs. Boom had provided Ginger Pop and a plate of macaroons. And Binnacle, the retired Pirate who did the Admiral's cooking and mending, had allowed them to look at the Skull and Crossbones tattooed upon his chest.

Yes, thought Michael, looking down at the bottle, it had really been a lovely day.

Then, aloud, he said wistfully, "I wish *I* could have a Glass of Port. I'm sure it must be delicious!"

"Step up, please!" Mary Poppins commanded. "And don't keep scratching at that label, Michael! You are not a Tufted Woodpecker!"

"I can't step up any quicker!" he grumbled. "And why must we hurry, Mary Poppins?" He was thinking that when the bottle was empty he would make a ship to put in it.

"We are hurrying," said Mary Poppins, with awful distinctness, "because this is the Second Thursday and I am going out."

"Oh!" groaned Michael, who had quite forgotten. "That means an evening with Ellen!"

He looked at Jane for sympathy but Jane took no notice. She was holding her Cowrie Shell to her ear and listening to the sound of the sea.

"I can't bear Ellen!" Michael grumbled. "She's always got a cold and her feet are too big."

"I wish I could *see* the Sea!" Jane murmured, as she peered inside the shell.

Mary Poppins gave an impatient snort. "There you go! Wish, wish, wishing — all day long! If it isn't a Glass of Port, it's the Sea! I never knew such a pair for wishing!"

"Well, you never *need* to wish!" said Michael. "You're perfect, just as you are!"

She'll be pleased with that, he thought to himself, as he gave her a flattering smile.

"Humph!" said her disbelieving look. But a dimple danced suddenly into her cheek.

"Get along with you, Michael Banks!" she cried, and hustled them through the gate. . . .

It turned out later, to Michael's surprise, that Ellen had no cold. She had another ailment, however, which went by the name of 'Ay Fever. She sneezed and sneezed till her face grew red. And it seemed to Michael that her feet grew bigger.

"I'm afraid I'll sneeze me 'ead right off!" she said lugubriously. And Michael almost wished she would.

"If there weren't any Thursdays," he said to Jane, "Mary Poppins would *never* go out!"

But, unfortunately, every week had a Thursday and once Mary Poppins was out of the house, it was no good calling her back.

There she went now, tripping down the Lane. She wore her black straw hat with the daisies and her best blue coat with the silver buttons. The children leaned from the nursery window and watched her retreating back. The parrot-head of her umbrella had a perky look, and she walked with a jaunty, expectant air as though she knew that a pleasant surprise awaited her round the corner.

"I wonder where she's going!" said Jane.

"I wish I were going, too!" groaned Michael. "Oh, Ellen, can't you stop sneezing!"

"Colder-hearted than a Toad, that boy is!" observed Ellen to her handkerchief. "As if I did it for choice! A-tishoo!"

She sneezed till the nursery furniture trembled. She sneezed the afternoon away and she sneezed all through supper. She sneezed the five of them through their baths and put them into bed, still sneezing. Then she sneezed on the night-light, sneezed the door shut and sneezed herself down the stairs.

"Thank goodness!" said Michael. "Now, let's do something!"

If Mary Poppins had been on duty they would never have dared to do anything. But nobody took any notice of Ellen.

Jane pattered over to the mantelpiece and took down the Cowrie Shell.

"It's still going on!" she said with delight. "Singing and gently roaring!"

"Good Gracious!" cried Michael, as he, too, listened. "I can even hear the fish swimming!"

"Don't be so silly! What nonsense you talk! Nobody ever heard a fish swim!"

Jane and Michael glanced round hurriedly. Whose voice was that? And where did it come from?

"Well, don't stand goggling at each other! Come on in!" the strange voice cried. And this time it seemed to come from the Shell.

"It's perfectly simple! Just shut your eyes and hold your breath — and dive!"

"Dive where?" said Michael disbelievingly. "We don't want to hit our heads on the hearth-rug!"

"Hearth-rug? Don't be so silly! Dive!" the voice commanded again.

"Come on, Michael! Stand beside me! At least we can try!" said Jane.

So, holding the Cowrie Shell between them, they shut their eyes and drew in their breath and dived as the voice had told them. To their surprise, their heads hit nothing. But the roaring sound from the Shell grew louder and a wind ran swiftly by their cheeks. Down they went, swooping like a pair of swallows, till suddenly water splashed around them and a wave went over their heads.

Michael opened his mouth and gave a splutter. "Oh, oh!" he cried loudly, "it tastes of salt!"

"Well, what did you think it would taste of? Sugar?" said the same little voice beside them.

"Are you all right, Michael?" Jane called anxiously.

"Ye-yes," he said bravely. "As long as you're there!"

She seized his hand and they dived together through rising walls of water.

"Shan't be long now," the voice assured them. "I can see the lights already."

Lights in the water — how strange! thought Jane. And she opened her eyes for a peep.

Below shone a ripple of coloured flares — blue, rose and silver, scarlet and green.

"Pretty, aren't they?" said the voice in her ear. And, turning, she saw, looking gleefully at her, the round, bright eye of a Sea-Trout. He was perched like a bird on the bough of a tree, whose branches were all of crimson.

"That's coral!" she cried in astonishment. "We must be down in the deeps of the sea!"

"Well, wasn't that what you wanted?" said the Trout. "I thought you wished you could see the sea!"

"I did," said Jane, looking very surprised. "But I never expected the wish to come true."

"Great Oceans! Why bother to wish it, then? I call that simply a waste of time. But come on! We mustn't be late for the Party!"

And before they had time to wonder where the Party was, he swept away through forests of coral and they dived behind him with the greatest of ease.

"Jumping Jellyfish!" cried a frightened voice. "What a start you gave me! It looked like a net!" A large fish darted through a curl of Jane's hair and hurtled away, looking very upset.

"That's the Haddock. He's nervous," the Trout explained. "He's lost so many old friends up there——"

he pointed his fin up through the water, "and he's always afraid it's his turn next."

Jane thought how often she had eaten haddock for breakfast and felt a little guilty.

"I'm sorry —— " she began to say, when a loud rough voice interrupted her.

"Move along, please! Don't block up the sea-lanes! Why can't you keep your fins to yourself!" A huge Cod shouldered his way between them.

"Cluttering up the Ocean like this! It's disgraceful! I'll be late for the Party!" He flung an angry glance at the children. "And who are you, anyway?" he demanded.

They were just about to tell him their names when the Trout swam up beside the Cod and whispered in his ear.

"Oh, I see! Well, I hope they've got money to pay for their tickets!"

"Well — no —— " Jane fumbled in her pocket.

"Tch, tch, tch! It's always the way. No method in anyone's madness. Here!" The Cod whisked a couple of flat white discs from a pocket under his tail. "Sand dollars," he explained importantly. "I always keep a few about me. Never know when I may need 'em." He tossed the dollars at the children and floundered away through the coral.

"Silly Old Codger!" remarked the Trout. "You needn't worry about your tickets. You're Guests of Honour. You'll get in free."

Jane and Michael looked at each other in surprise. They

had never before been guests of honour and they felt very proud and superior.

"*Who'll* get in free, I'd like to know? Nobody's going to get in free while I'm around in the Ocean. Nor out, either, if it comes to that!" a grating, sawlike voice informed them.

Jane and Michael spun round. A pair of staring eyes met theirs, and a set of hairy, hungry feelers reached out in every direction. It was an Octopus.

"Yum, yu-u-um!" said the Octopus, leering at Michael. "Bobby Shafto's fat and fair — and just what I need for my Supper!" He reached out one of the dreadful feelers and Michael gave a squeak of terror.

"Oh, no, you don't!" the Trout said quickly. And he whispered a word to the Octopus as Jane whisked Michael away.

"What? Speak up, can't you? I'm hard of hearing! Oh, I see. They belong to — all right, all right!"

The Octopus drew in his feeler regretfully. "We are always delighted," he went on loudly, "to have among us at High Tide anybody belonging to —— "

"What in the Sea is all that chatter? I never get a moment's peace!" a querulous voice broke in.

The children turned in its direction. But all they saw was one small claw waving from inside a shell.

"That's the Hermit Crab!" the Trout explained. "Lives by himself and does nothing but grumble. Shuts up like a clam if anyone speaks to him. But, come! We must hurry. The music's starting."

Soft sounds of music came to their ears as they followed him through a tunnel of rock. A faint glow shone at the end of the tunnel and the music grew louder as they swam towards it. Then suddenly their eyes were dazzled as a flood of brilliance broke upon them. They had reached the end of the shadowy tunnel and before them was the loveliest sight the children had ever seen.

There lay the stretching floor of the sea, sown with soft lawns of greenest seaweed. It was threaded with paths of golden sand and dappled with flowers of every colour. Up from the sand stretched trees of coral, and plumes of sea-fern lolled on the water. The dark rocks glittered with shining shells and one of them, the largest of all, was covered with mother-of-pearl. Behind this rock lay a deep dark cavern, as black as the sky on a moonless night. And far within it faint lights twinkled as though stars shone in the depths of the sea.

Jane and Michael, at the tunnel's edge, looked out and gasped with delight.

Nothing in that bright scene was still. The rocks themselves seemed to bow and swing in the endless ripple of water. The small fish fluttered like butterflies between the swaying flowers. And festoons of seaweed, slung from the coral, were hung with a thousand swinging lights.

Chinese lanterns! thought Jane to herself. But, looking closer, she saw that the lights were really luminous fish. They hung by their mouths from the strings of seaweed and lit up the lawns with their brightness.

The music was playing more loudly now. It came from a little terrace of coral where several Crabs were playing on fiddles. A Flounder was puffing out its cheeks and blowing down a conch shell; while Cornet fish played on silver cornets and a Bass beat time on a big bass drum. About the players swam the bright sea-creatures, darting between the rock and the coral and leaping and plunging in time with the music. Mermaids in necklaces of pearl swam daintily round among the fish. And the silver sheen of tail and fin went sparkling everywhere.

"Oh!" cried Jane and Michael together, for it seemed the only thing to say.

"Well, here you are at last!" said a booming voice, as a big Bronze Seal came flapping towards them. "You're just in time for the Garden Party." He offered a flipper to each of the children and waddled along between them.

"Do you often give Garden Parties?" asked Michael. He was wishing he, too, could live in the sea.

"Oh, dear me, no!" the Seal replied. "Only when High Tide falls on — I say! I say! Were you invited?" He broke off to speak to a large grey shape. "I was told no whales were to be admitted!"

"Get out! Get out! No whales allowed!" came a chorus of fishy voices.

The Whale gave a flick of his monstrous tail and darted between two rocks. He had a large pathetic face and great sad eyes which he turned on the children.

"It's the same each time," he said, shaking his head. "They say I'm too big, and I eat too much. Can't *you* persuade them to make an Exception? I do want to see the Distant Relative!"

"Whose distant relative?" Jane began, when the Seal interrupted loudly.

"Now, don't be pathetic, Whale. Get moving! Remember the last Unfortunate Incident. He ate up all the Sardine Sandwiches," the Seal said to Jane behind his flipper.

"No Admission Except on Business. All Riff-Raff keep outside the gates. Off with you, now. Swim along! No nonsense!" A fish with a sharp sword on his nose came bustling across the lawns.

"I never have any fun!" blubbered the Whale, as the Seal and the Swordfish chased him away.

Jane felt very sorry for him. "But, after all," she said, turning to Michael, "he does take up a lot of space!"

But Michael was no longer beside her. He had swum away with one of the mermaids who was dabbing at her face with a little pink sponge.

"Well, skirts, I suppose. And blouses and boots," Jane heard him saying as she swam towards them.

The Mermaid turned to Jane and smiled. "I was asking him about fashions up there —— " she nodded upwards through the sea, "and he says they are wearing blouses and boots." She spoke the words with a little laugh as though they could not be true.

"And coats," Jane added. "And galoshes, of course!"

"Galoshes?" The Mermaid raised her eyebrows.

"To keep our feet dry," Jane explained.

The Mermaid gave a trill of laughter. "How very extraordinary!" she said. "Down here, we prefer to keep everything wet!" She turned on her tail to swim away when a clear voice suddenly hailed her.

"Hullo, Anemone!" it cried. And out from behind a bed of lilies a silver shape came leaping. At the sight of the children it stopped in mid-water and stared at them with its great bright eyes. "Why, Bless my Sole!" it cried in surprise. "Whoever caught those creatures?"

"Nobody," tinkled the Mermaid gaily, as she whispered behind her hand.

"Oh, really? How very delightful!" said the fish, with a supercilious smile.

"I suppose I should introduce myself. I'm the Deep-Sea Salmon," he explained, preening his silver fins. "King of the Fish, you know, and all that. I dare say you've heard of me now and again!" Indeed, by the way he swaggered and preened, you would have thought there was nothing else worth hearing about!

"Refreshments! Refreshments!" said a gloomy voice, as a Pike, with the air of an elderly butler, came hovering past with a tray.

"Help yourself!" said the Salmon, bowing to Jane, "A Sardine Sandwich or a Salted Shrimp? Or Jelly — the fishy kind, of course! And what about you —— ?" he turned to

Michael. "Some Sea-Cow milk or Barnacle Beer? Or perhaps you'd prefer just Plain Sea Water!"

"I was given to h'understand, your 'Ighness, that the h'young gentleman h'wished for Port!" The Pike stared before him gloomily as he held out the tray towards them.

"Then Port he shall have!" said the Salmon imperiously, as he whisked a dark red drink from the tray.

With a start of surprise, Michael remembered his wish. He took the glass and sipped it eagerly. "It's igzactly like Raspberry Fizz!" he cried.

"Good!" said the Salmon conceitedly, as though he had made the Port himself. "Now, how would you like to look at the Catch? They're probably reeling the last ones in and we'll just have time if we hurry!"

"I wonder what has been caught!" thought Jane, as they darted along beside the Salmon. The sea-lanes by now were crowded with fish who were leaping towards the lawn.

"Now! Now! Remember whom you're pushing!" said the Salmon in a haughty voice as he scattered them right and left. "My Fins and Flippers! Look at those children!" He pointed to a group of Sea-Urchins who were tumbling noisily by. "Schoolmaster! Keep an eye on your pupils! This Ocean's becoming an absolute Bear Garden!"

"Eh what?" said an absent-minded fish who was floating along with his nose in a book. "Here, Winkle and Twinkle!

And you, too, Spiky! Behave — or I shan't let you go to the Party!"

The urchins looked at each other and grinned. Then they solemnly swam along with the Schoolmaster, looking as though butter wouldn't melt in their mouths.

"Ah, here we are!" cried the Salmon gaily, as he led the children round a cluster of coral.

On a large flat rock sat a row of fish, all solemnly staring upward. Each fish held a fishing-rod in his fin and watched his line with an earnest gaze as it ran up through the water.

"The Angler-fish," the Salmon explained. "Talk softly! They don't like to be disturbed."

"But——" whispered Jane, looking very surprised, "the lines are going upwards!"

The Salmon stared. "Where else would they go?" he wanted to know. "You could hardly expect them to go downwards, could you? Bait!" he added, pointing to several water-proof bags that were filled with pastry tarts.

"But — what do they catch?" whispered Michael hoarsely.

"Oh, humans, mostly," the Salmon replied. "You can get almost anyone with a Strawberry Tart. They've taken a pretty good catch already. Look at them squirming and twitching!"

He flicked his tail at a nearby cave and the children gasped with astonishment. For there, looking very cross and disgruntled, stood a cluster of human beings. Men in dark goggles and summer hats were shaking their fists and stamping. Three elderly ladies were waving umbrellas and a younger one in rubber boots was wringing her hands in despair. Beside her holding a shrimping net, stood two disconsolate children.

"Well, how do *you* like it?" jeered the Salmon. "I must say you look extremely funny! Exactly like fish out of water!"

The humans all gave a furious snort and turned their backs on the Salmon. And at the same moment, from somewhere above, a wild cry rent the sea.

"Let me go, I say! Take this hook out at once! How dare you do such a thing to me!"

One of the Angler-fish, smiling quietly, began to reel in his line.

"Take it out, I tell you!" came the voice again.

And down through the sea, with a rush of bubbles, came a most extraordinary figure. Its body was clothed in a thick tweed coat; a grey veil floated from the hat on its head; and upon its feet were thick wool stockings and large-size button boots.

Michael opened his mouth and stared and made a gargling noise.

"Jane! Do you see? I believe it's —— "

"Miss Andrew!" said Jane, who was gargling, too.

And Miss Andrew indeed it was. Down she came, coughing and choking and shouting. The Angler-fish

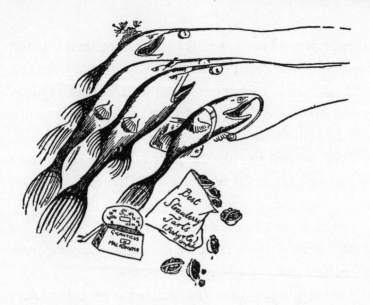

jerked the hook from her mouth and pushed her towards the cave.

"Outrageous! Preposterous!" she spluttered. "How was *I* to know that Tart had a hook on it! You villains!" She shook her fist at the Anglers. "I shall write to *The Times!* I shall have you fried!"

"Look at her writhing!" crowed the Salmon. "She's a whopper! She'll wriggle for hours and hours."

Jane felt that Miss Andrew deserved all she got, but she looked at the children anxiously. How terrible, she thought to herself, if *she* had been caught — or Michael!

"What will the Anglers do with them?" she asked the Salmon earnestly.

"Oh, throw them back again, of course! We only catch them for sport, you know. They're far too tough for eating."

"Hey! Come along, Salmon!" called the Seal from the distance. "We can't let the children miss the Greeting. And she's due to arrive any minute."

Jane looked at Michael in silent question. Who could *she* be? An important Mermaid? Or perhaps the Queen of the Sea!

"Kippers and Catfish! I'd forgotten! Come on, you two!" cried the Salmon.

He went before them, leaping and curving. Beside them a sea-horse trotted swiftly. And fish swam in and out among them as they hurried towards the lawns.

"Hullo, Jane and Michael!" piped a friendly voice. "Remember me — in your goldfish bowl? I'm back at home now. Give my love to your Mother!" The Goldfish smiled and darted away before they had time to answer.

"What a crush! One might as well be tinned!" said the Salmon, threshing his tail.

"Refreshments! Refreshments!" the Pike cried hoarsely.

"Yo, ho, ho! And a bottle of rum!" a familiar voice answered. And Admiral Boom came plunging past and seized a glass from the tray. Beside him swam Mrs. Boom's dove-like figure. And, floundering in their wake, came Binnacle.

"Shiver my timbers! Ahoy there, messmates! For I'm bound for the Rio Grande!" bawled the Admiral.

The Pike stared after him, shaking his head. "'Ooligans — that's what they are!" he said gloomily. "I h'really don't know h'what the h'Ocean's coming to!"

"Ah, there you are, children!" the Bronze Seal cried, as he shouldered his way through the throng. "Hang on to my tall and I'll pull you through. Excuse me! Let me pass, please, fish! These are Jane and Michael, the Guests of Honour!"

The fish drew back and stared at them. Polite murmurs of welcome sounded amid the noise. The Seal pushed the crowd aside with his flippers and dragged the children after him to the rock of shining pearl.

"We're just in time for the Greeting!" he panted. They could hardly hear his booming voice because of the shouting and laughter.

"What greeting?" Jane was about to ask, when, all of a sudden, the shouting ceased. The music and laughter died away and a deep hush fell on the sea. Each fish in the crowd was as still as stone. The swaying flowers stood quiet in the water. And the tide itself was still.

"He's coming!" said the Seal in a whisper, as he nodded towards the cave.

"He's coming!" the watching creatures echoed.

Then, out from the black mysterious cave, a withered head emerged. A pair of ancient sleepy eyes blinked at the dazzle of lights. Two wrinkled flippers stretched from the darkness and a domed black shell heaved up behind them.

The children clutched the Bronze Seal's flippers.

"Who is it?" whispered Jane in his ear. She thought it might be a tortoise, perhaps, or a strange kind of turtle.

"The Terrapin," the Seal replied gruffly. "The oldest and wisest thing in the world."

Inch by inch on trembling flippers the Terrapin crept to the pearly rock. His eyes beneath the half-closed lids were like two small black stars. He gazed at the assembled creatures for a moment. Then lifting his withered, ancient head the Terrapin smiled, and spoke.

"My friends," he began majestically, in a voice like an old, cracked bell, "I greet you, creatures of the Sea! And I wish you a happy High-Tide Party!"

He bowed his withered head to the rock and the fish bowed humbly in the water.

"This is a great occasion for us all," the Terrapin went on quietly. "I am glad indeed to see tonight so many old acquaintances." His black-star gaze swept the crowded lawns, as though in one glance he recognized every creature in the sea. "But surely," the wrinkled brows went up, "there is one of us missing!"

The Seal glanced round towards the tunnel and his voice boomed out with a cry of triumph.

"She is here, my lord! She has just arrived!"

As he spoke a clamour of voices rose and the creatures clapped and cheered. At the same moment, to the children's amazement, a figure that was strangely familiar appeared at the edge of the tunnel. There it stood, dressed in its best blue coat and the straw hat trimmed with daisies. Then, dainty and graceful, neat and prim, it swooped across the shining gardens. The cheering rose to a roar of joy as it landed upon the Terrapin's rock.

"Welcome, Mary Poppins!" cried a thousand happy voices.

She waved her parrot umbrella in greeting, then she turned and curtsied to the Terrapin.

For a long moment he gazed at her, as though his ancient glittering eyes were looking into her heart. Then he waved his little naked head and gave her a friendly smile.

"My dear young relative!" he said, graciously. "This is indeed a pleasure. It is long since I had a visitor from the world above the water. And long, too, since your Second Thursday fell upon our High Tide. Therefore, in the name of the creatures of the deep, I bid you welcome, Mary!" And, blinking, he offered her a small withered flipper.

Mary Poppins took it and bowed respectfully. Then the china blue eyes looked into the black ones and a strange smile passed between them. It was as though neither of them had any secrets from the other.

"And now, dear Mary," the Terrapin continued, "since nobody comes down to the depths of the sea without taking something away with them, let me give you a little present."

He reached his flipper back into the cave and brought out a small bright object. "Take this to remind you of your visit. It will make a nice brooch, or perhaps a hat-pin." And, leaning forward, he pressed a starfish on Mary Poppins' coat. It shone and twinkled upon the blue like a little cluster of diamonds.

"Oh, thank you!" she said, with a cry of delight. "It's exactly what I wanted!"

She smiled at the Terrapin and then at the star and her glance slid away to the children. The smile faded instantly. She gave a disgusted sniff.

"If I've told you once, Jane, not to gape, I've told you a thousand times! Close your mouth, Michael! You are not a Codfish!"

"I should think not!" muttered the Cod indignantly, from his place behind the children.

"So — these are Jane and Michael!" said the Terrapin, as he turned his sleepy eyes upon them. "I am very glad to meet you at last. Welcome, my children, to our High-Tide Party!"

He bowed gravely and, urged by Mary Poppins' glare, they bowed in return. "You see," he went on in his old, cracked voice, "I know who Jane and Michael are. But I wonder — yes, I wonder indeed, if *they* know who *I* am!"

They shook their heads and gazed at him speechlessly.

He moved his carapace a little and thoughtfully blinked for a moment. Then he spoke.

"I am the Terrapin. I dwell at the roots of the world. Under the cities, under the hills, under the very sea itself, I make my home. Up from my dark root, through the waters, the earth rose with its flowers and forests. The man and the mountain sprang from it. The great beasts, too, and the birds of the air."

He ceased for a moment and the creatures in the sea

about him were quiet as they watched him. Then he went on. "I am older than all things that are. Silent and dark and wise am I, and quiet and very patient. Here in my cave all things have their beginning. And all things return to me in the end. I can wait. I can wait . . ."

He folded his lids upon his eyes and nodded his naked wrinkled head as though he were talking to himself. "I have no more to say," he said, blinking. "So —— " he held up a little lordly flipper. "Bid the music play!" he commanded the Seal. "And let the sea-people choose their dance. What shall it be this time, my children?"

"Tiddy-um-pom-pom, tiddy-um-pom-pom!" hummed a voice like a bee in a bottle.

"Ah, yes, my dear Admiral!" the Terrapin nodded. "A very suitable suggestion. Strike up the Sailor's Hornpipe!"

At once a wild commotion rose. The band broke into swift gay music and the still fish flickered their tails again. Voices and laughter filled the sea and the tide began to move.

Tiddy-um-pom-pom! Away they went — fishes and mermaids, urchins, seals.

Tiddy-um-pom-pom! cried Admiral Boom, as he pulled on invisible tarry ropes. Tiddy-um-pom-pom! sang Mrs. Boom, clasping her hands and rocking her feet. Tiddy-um-pom-pom! sang Binnacle loudly, as he thought of his happy pirate days. And the fish danced in and out among them and waved their shining fins.

The Bronze Seal flapped up and down on his tail and the Salmon swooped over the lawns like a bird. The Angler-fish pranced by with their rods and the Swordfish and School-master danced together. And ever among the scaly throng, a dark shape moved like a graceful shadow. Heel and toe, went Mary Poppins as she danced the Hornpipe on the floor of the sea.

The children stood by the pearly rock and stared at the curious scene.

"You find it strange, do you not?" said the Terrapin. "I can see you are feeling all at sea!" He cackled gently at his own little joke.

Jane nodded. "I thought the sea would be so different, but really, it's very like the land!"

"And why not?" said the Terrapin, blinking. "The land came out of the sea, remember. Each thing on the earth has a brother here — the lion, the dog, the hare, the elephant. The precious gems have their kind in the sea, so have the starry constellations. The rose remembers the salty waters and the moon the ebb and flow of the tide. You, too, must remember it, Jane and Michael! There are more things in the sea, my children, than ever came out of it. And I don't mean fish!" the Terrapin smiled. "But I see that your twenty toes are twitching! Be off with you, now, and join the dance."

Jane seized Michael by the hand. Then, because she remembered he was very old, she curtsied to the Terrapin before they darted away.

"Tiddy-um-pom-pom!"

They plunged together among the fish in time to the beat of the music. Oh, how their bare feet twinkled and pranced! Oh, how their arms waved through the water! And their bodies swayed like strands of seaweed as they went through the steps of the Sailor's Hornpipe.

Tiddy-um-pom-pom! cried the merry music, as Mary Poppins came swimming towards them. She took their hands and they danced together, pulling and rocking through the boughs of coral. Round they went, faster and ever faster, spinning like tops in the spinning water. Till, dazed with the dance and dazzled with lights, they closed their eyes and leaned against her. And her arms went round them, firmly, strongly, as she lifted them through the moving tide.

Tiddy-um-pom-pom! They swung together and the music grew fainter as they swung. Tiddy-um-pom-pom! Oh, the circling sea, that rocks us all in its mighty cradle! Tiddy-um-pom-pom! Oh, Mary Poppins, swing me round like a bubble in the falling tide. Swing me round — tiddy-um . . . Swing me round — pom-pom . . . Swing me . . . Swing me . . . Swing. . . .

"Hold me tight, Mary Poppins!" murmured Michael drowsily, as he felt for her comforting arm.

There was no answer.

"Are you there, Mary Poppins?" he said with a yawn, as he leaned on the rocking sea.

Still no answer.

So, keeping his eyes closed, he called again and the sea seemed to echo his voice. "Mary Poppins, I want you! Mary Poppins, where are you?"

"Where I always am at this hour of the morning!" she replied with an angry snap.

"Oh, what a beautiful dance!" he said sleepily. And he put out his hand to draw her to him.

It touched nothing. All that his searching fingers found was a warm, soft bulkiness suspiciously like a pillow.

"I'll thank you to dance yourself out of bed! It is nearly time for breakfast!"

Her voice had the rumble of distant thunder. And Michael opened his eyes with a start.

Good gracious! Where was he? Surely it could not be the Nursery! Yet there was Old Dobbin standing still in the corner; and Mary Poppins' neat camp bed and the toys and the books and his slippers. All the old familiar things were there but the last thing Michael wanted just now was an old familiar thing.

"But where's the sea gone?" he said crossly. "I want to be back in the sea!"

Her face popped round the bathroom door and he knew at once she was furious.

"The sea is at Brighton where it always is!" she said, with fierce distinctness. "Now, spit-spot and up you get. And Not Another Word!"

"But I was in it a moment ago! And so were you, Mary Poppins. We were dancing around among the fish and doing the Sailor's Hornpipe!"

"Humph!" she said, giving the bath-mat a shake. "I hope I have something better to do than to go out dancing with sailors!"

"Well, what about all the fish?" he demanded. "And the Seal and the Salmon and that funny old Turtle? We were down there with them, Mary Poppins, right on the floor of the sea!"

"Down in the sea? With a funny old Salmon? Well, you certainly have the fishiest dreams! I suppose you had too many buns for Supper! Sailors and Turtles, indeed! What next?" Her apron gave an angry crackle as she flounced away, muttering.

He gazed at her retreating back and frowned and shook his head. He dared not say any more, he knew, but she couldn't stop him wondering.

So he wondered and wondered as he got out of bed and poked his toes into his slippers. And as he wondered his eyes met Jane's as she peeped from under the blankets. She had heard every word of the argument and while she had listened, she had thought her own thoughts and her eyes had noticed something. Now she smiled a secret smile at Michael and nodded her head wisely.

"It was fishy," she said. "But it wasn't a dream." And she pointed to the mantelpiece.

He looked up. He gave a start of surprise. Then a smile of triumph spread over his face.

For there, beside the Cowrie Shell, were the two Sand Dollars and a little pink Starfish.

"You remember what the Terrapin said? Everyone who goes down to the sea brings something back," Jane reminded him.

Michael nodded as he gazed at the Sand Dollars. And at that moment the door burst open and Mary Poppins bounced back. She plucked the Starfish from the mantelpiece and pinned it to her collar. It twinkled brightly as she prinked and pranked in front of the Nursery mirror.

Michael turned to Jane with a smothered giggle.

"Tiddy-um-pom-pom!" he hummed under his breath.

"Tiddy-um-pom-pom!" Jane said in a whisper.

And, daringly, behind Mary Poppins' stiff straight back, they danced a few steps of the Hornpipe.

They never noticed that her bright blue eyes were watching them in the mirror and calmly exchanging with her own reflection a very superior smile. . . .

CHAPTER SEVEN

Happy Ever After

I t was the last day of the Old Year.

Upstairs in the Nursery, Jane and Michael and the Twins were going through that magical performance known as Undressing. When Mary Poppins set to work, it was almost as good as watching a Conjuror!

She moved along the row of children and their clothes seemed to fall away at her touch. Over John's head she pulled the sweater as quickly as though she were skinning a rabbit. Jane's frock dropped off at a single touch; Barbara's socks literally ran off her toes. As for Michael, he always felt that Mary Poppins undressed him simply by giving him one of her looks.

"Now, spit-spot into bed!" she ordered.

And with the words went such a glare that they fled squealing in all directions and darted under the bedclothes.

She moved about the Nursery, folding up the scattered clothes and tidying the toys. The children lay cosily in their beds, watching the crackling wing of her apron as it whisked about the room. Her eyes were blue and her cheeks were pink and her nose turned up with a perky air like the nose of a Dutch Doll. To look at her, they thought to themselves, you would never imagine she was anything but a perfectly ordinary person. But, as you know and I know, they had every reason to believe that Appearances are Deceptive.

Suddenly Michael had an idea that seemed to him very important.

"I say!" he said, sitting up in bed. "When igzackly does the Old Year end?"

"Tonight," said Mary Poppins shortly. "At the first stroke of twelve."

"And when does it begin?" he went on.

"When does what begin?" she snapped.

"The New Year," answered Michael patiently.

"On the last stroke of twelve," she replied, giving a short sharp sniff.

"Oh? Then what happens in between?" he demanded.

"Between what? Can't you speak properly, Michael? Do you think I'm a Mind Reader?"

He wanted to say Yes, for that was exactly what he did think. But he knew he would never dare.

"Between the first and the last stroke," he explained hurriedly.

Mary Poppins turned and glared at him.

"Never trouble Trouble till Trouble troubles you!" she advised priggishly.

"But I'm not troubling Trouble, Mary Poppins. I was only wanting to know——" he broke off quickly, for Mary Poppins' face had a Very Ominous look.

"Then Want must be your Master. Now! If I have One More Word from you——" At the sound of that phrase he dived under the blankets. For he knew very well what it meant.

Mary Poppins gave another sniff and moved along the row of beds, tucking them all in.

"I'll take that, thank you!" she remarked, as she plucked the Blue Duck from John's arms.

"Oh, *no!*" cried John. "Please give him to me!"

"I want my Monkey!" Barbara wailed, as Mary Poppins uncurled her fingers from the moth-eaten body of Pinnie. Pinnie was an old rag Monkey who had belonged first to Mrs. Banks when she was a little girl, and then to each of the children in turn.

But Mary Poppins took no notice. She hurried on to Jane's bed and Alfred, the grey-flannel Elephant, was plucked from under the blankets. Jane sat up quickly.

"But why are you taking the toys?" she demanded. "Can't we sleep with them as we always do?"

Mary Poppins' only answer was an icy glare flung over her shoulder as she stooped to Michael's bed.

"The Pig, please!" she commanded, sternly. She put out her hand for the small, gilt cardboard Pig that Aunt Flossie had given him for Christmas.

At first the Pig had been filled with chocolates but now he was quite empty. A large hole yawned in the back of his body at the place where the tail should have been. On Christmas Day Michael had wrenched it off to see how it was stuck on. Since then it had lain on the mantelpiece and the Pig had gone without it.

Michael clutched the Golden Pig in his arms.

"No, Mary Poppins!" he said bravely. "He's *my* Pig! And I want him!"

"*What did I say?*" asked Mary Poppins. And her look was so awful that Michael loosened his hold at once and let her take it from him.

"But what are you going to do with them?" he asked curiously.

For Mary Poppins was arranging the animals in a row on top of the toy-cupboard.

"Ask no Questions and you'll be Told no Lies," she retorted priggishly. Her apron gave another crackle as she crossed the room to the book-case.

They watched her take down three well-known books: *Robinson Crusoe, The Green Fairy Book* and *Mother Goose Nursery Rhymes*. Then she opened them and laid them down in front of the four animals.

Does she mean the animals to read the books? Jane wondered to herself.

"And now," said Mary Poppins, primly, as she moved towards the door, "turn over, all of you — if you please — and go to sleep at once!"

Michael sat bolt upright.

"But I want to stay awake, Mary Poppins, and watch for the New Year!"

"A Watched Pot Never Boils!" she reminded him. "Lie down, please, Michael, in that bed — and don't say Another Word!"

Then, sniffing loudly, she snapped out the light, and shut the Nursery door behind her with an angry little click.

"I will watch all the same," said Michael, as soon as she had gone.

"So will I," agreed Jane quickly, with a very determined air.

The Twins said nothing. They were fast asleep. But it was at least ten minutes before Michael's head fell sideways on his pillow. And quite fifteen before Jane's eyelashes fluttered down on her cheeks.

The four eiderdowns rose and fell with the children's steady breathing.

For a long time nothing stirred the silence of the Nursery.

Ding-dong! Ding-dong! Ding-dong! Ding-dong!

Suddenly, through the silent night, a peal of bells rang out.

Ding-dong! Ring-ting! Ding-dong!

From every tower and steeple the swinging chimes went forth. The bells of the city echoed and tossed and floated across the Park to the Lane. From North and South and East and West they pealed and clanged and chimed. People leaned over their window-sills and rattled their dinner bells. And those who hadn't a dinner bell played tunes on their Front Door knockers.

Along the Lane came the Ice Cream Man, twanging his bicycle bell with gusto. In the garden of Admiral Boom, at the corner, a ship's bell clanged through the frosty air. And Miss Lark, in the Next Door drawing-room, tinkled her little breakfast bell, while the two dogs barked and howled.

Clang-clang! Tinkle-tinkle! Ding-dong! Bow-wow!

Everybody in the world was ringing a bell. The echoes clashed and chimed and rhymed in the chilly midnight dark.

Then all of a sudden, there was silence. And out of the stillness, solemn and deep, the sound of a great clock striking.

"Boom!" said Big Ben.

It was the first stroke of Midnight.

At that moment something stirred in the Nursery. Then came the sound of clattering hooves.

Jane and Michael were wide awake in an instant. They both sat up with a start.

"Goodness!" said Michael.

"Gracious!" said Jane.

For before them lay an astounding sight. There on the floor, stood the Golden Pig, prancing about on his gold hind trotters and looking very important.

Plump! With a heavy muffled thud, Alfred the Elephant landed beside him. And, leaping lightly from the top of the cupboard, came Pinnie the Monkey and the old Blue Duck.

Then, to the children's astonishment, the Golden Pig spoke.

"Will somebody kindly put on my tail?" he enquired in a high, shrill voice.

Michael flung himself out of bed and rushed to the mantelpiece.

"That's better," remarked the Pig, with a smile. "I've been most uncomfortable ever since Christmas. A Pig without a tail, you know, is almost as bad as a tail without a Pig. And now," he went on, as he glanced round the room, "are we all ready? Then, hurry, please!"

As he spoke he pranced daintily to the door, followed by Alfred, Pinnie and the Duck.

"Where are you going?" Jane cried, staring.

"You'll soon see," answered the Pig. "Come on!"

In a flash they had flung on gowns and slippers and were following the four toys down the stairs and out through their own Front Door.

"This way!" said the Pig, as he pranced across Cherry-Tree Lane and through the Gates of the Park.

Pinnie and the Blue Duck danced beside him, wildly squealing and quacking. And after them lumbered Alfred the Elephant with Jane and Michael at his grey-flannel heels.

Above the trees hung a round white moon. Its gleaming silver rays poured down on the wide lawns of the Park. And there on the grass was a throng of figures, moving backwards and forwards in the shimmering light.

Alfred flung up his flannel trunk and eagerly sniffed the air.

"Ha!" he remarked delightedly. "We're safely inside, Pig, don't you think?"

"Inside what?" asked Michael curiously.

"The Crack," said Alfred, flapping his ears.

The children stared at each other. What on earth could Alfred mean?

But the Pig was beckoning them towards him with a wave of his golden trotter; and bright forms flickered behind and around them as they hurried to the lawn.

"Excuse us, please!" said three small shapes as they brushed against the children.

"The Three Blind Mice," explained Alfred, smiling. "They're always under everyone's feet!"

"Are they running away from the Farmer's Wife?" cried Michael, very surprised and excited.

"Oh, dear no! Not tonight," said Alfred. "They're hurrying to meet her. The Three Blind Mice and the Farmer's Wife are all inside the Crack!"

"Hullo, Alfred — you got in safely!"

"Why, it's dear old Pinnie!"

"What, the Blue Duck, too?"

"Hooray, hooray! Here's the Golden Pig!"

There were cries of welcome and shouts of joy as everyone greeted everyone else. A Tin Soldier who was marching past, saluted the Pig and he waved his trotter. Pinnie shook hands with a pair of birds whom he hailed as Cock Robin and Jenny Wren. And the Blue Duck quacked at an Easter Chicken half-in and half-out of its egg. As for Alfred, he flung up his trunk in all directions and loudly trumpeted greetings.

"Aren't you cold, my dear? It's chilly tonight!" A gruff voice spoke behind Jane's shoulder.

She turned to find a bearded man dressed in the strangest garments. He had goatskin trousers, a beaver cap and a large umbrella of rabbit-tails. Behind him, with an armful of furs, stood a black, half-naked figure.

"Friday," said the bearded man. "Oblige me by giving this lady a coat."

"Suttinly, Massa! Ah aims to please!" And the great black creature, with a graceful movement, flung a sealskin cloak about Jane's shoulders.

She stared.

"So you're —— " she began, and smiled at him shyly.

"Of course I am," said the tall man, bowing. "Please call me Robinson! All my friends do. Mr. Crusoe sounds so formal."

"But I thought you were in a book!" said Jane.

"I am," said Robinson Crusoe, smiling. "But tonight someone kindly left it open. And so I escaped, you see!"

Jane thought of the books on top of the toy-cupboard. She remembered how Mary Poppins had opened them before she put out the light.

"Does it often happen?" she questioned eagerly.

"Alas, no! Only at the end of the year. The Crack's

our one and only chance. But, excuse me! I must speak
to —— "

Robinson Crusoe turned to greet a curious egg-shaped
little man who was hurrying past on spindly legs. His
pointed head was as bald as an egg and his neck was muffled in a woolen scarf. He stared inquisitively at the children, as he greeted Robinson Crusoe.

"Good Gracious!" cried Michael in surprise. "You're
igzackly like Humpty-Dumpty!"

"Like?" shrilled the little man, haughtily. "How can anyone be like himself, I'd like to know? I've heard of people
being *un*like themselves — when they've been naughty or
eaten too much — but never like. Don't be so silly!"

"But — you're quite whole!" said Michael, staring. "I
thought Humpty-Dumpty couldn't be mended."

"Who said I couldn't?" cried the little man, angrily.

"Well, I just thought — er — that all the King's horses
and — er — all the King's men —— " Michael began to
stammer.

"Pooh — horses! What do they know about it? And as
for the King's men — stupid creatures! — they only know
about horses! And because *they* couldn't put me together,
it doesn't say no one else could, does it?"

Not wishing to contradict him, Jane and Michael shook
their heads.

"As a matter of fact," Humpty-Dumpty went on, "the
King himself mended me — didn't you — heh?"

He shrieked the last words at a round fat man who was holding a crown on his head with one hand and carrying a pie-dish in the other.

"He's just like the King in Mary Poppins' story! He must be Old King Cole!" said Jane.

"Didn't I what?" the King enquired, carefully balancing his pie and his crown.

"Stick me together!" shrieked Humpty-Dumpty.

"Of course I did. Just for tonight, you know. With honey. In the Queen's parlour. But you really mustn't bother me now. My Four-and-Twenty Blackbirds are going to sing and I have to open the Pie."

"There, what did I tell you?" screamed Humpty-Dumpty. "How dare you suggest I'm a Broken Egg!" He turned his back upon them rudely and his big cracked head shone white in the moonlight.

"Don't argue with him! It's no good," said Alfred. "He's always so touchy about that fall. Here! Step on your own

toes! Look who you're pushing!" He turned and made a
sweep with his trunk and a crowned Lion lightly leapt
aside.

"Sorry!" exclaimed the Lion, politely. "It's such a frightful crush tonight. Have you seen the Unicorn, by the way?
Ah, there he is! Hi! Wait a minute!" And, growling softly in
his throat, he pounced upon a silvery figure that was daintily trotting by.

"Oh, stop him! Stop him!" Jane cried anxiously. "He's
going to beat the Unicorn all round the Town!"

"Not tonight," said Alfred, reassuringly. "You just watch!"

Jane and Michael stared with astonishment as they saw
the Lion bowing. Then he took the golden crown from his
head and offered it to the Unicorn.

"It's your turn to wear it," the Lion said courteously.

Then the two exchanged a tender embrace and danced off into the crowd.

"Children behaving nicely tonight?" they heard the Unicorn enquire of a withered old woman who was dancing past. She was pulling along an enormous Shoe, full of laughing boys and girls.

"Oh, *so* nicely!" cried the Old Woman gaily. "I haven't used my whip once! George Porgie is *such* a help with the girls. They *insist* on being kissed tonight. And as for the boys, they're just *sugar* and spice. *Look* at Red Riding Hood hugging that Wolf! She's trying to teach him to *beg* for supper. Sit down, please, Muffet. And hold on *tight!*"

The Old Woman waved at a fair little girl who sat at the back of the Shoe. She was deep in conversation with a large black Spider; and as the Shoe went rumbling past, she reached out her hand and patted him gently.

"She's not even running away!" cried Michael. "Why isn't she frightened?" he wanted to know.

"Because of the Crack," said Alfred again, as he hurried them before him.

Jane and Michael couldn't help staring at Red Riding Hood and Miss Muffett. Fancy not being afraid of the Wolf and that black enormous Spider!

Then a filmy whiteness brushed them lightly and they turned to find a shining shape yawning behind its hand.

"Still sleepy, Beauty?" trumpeted Alfred, as he slipped his trunk round her waist.

She patted the trunk and leaned against him.

"I was deep in a dream," she murmured softly. "But the First Stroke, luckily, woke me up!"

As she said that, Michael's curiosity could contain itself no longer.

"But I don't understand!" he burst out loudly. "Everything's upside down tonight! Why doesn't the Spider frighten Miss Muffett? And the Lion beat the Unicorn?"

"Alfred has told you," said Sleeping Beauty. "Because we are all in the Crack."

"*What* crack?" demanded Michael.

"The Crack between the Old Year and the New. The Old Year dies on the First Stroke of Midnight and the New Year is born on the Last Stroke. And in between — while the other ten strokes are sounding — there lies the secret Crack."

"Yes?" said Jane, breathlessly, for she wanted to know more.

The Sleeping Beauty gave a charming yawn and smiled upon the children.

"And inside the Crack all things are as one. The eternal opposites meet and kiss. The wolf and the lamb lie down together, the dove and the serpent share one nest. The stars bend down and touch the earth and the young and the old forgive each other. Night and day meet here, so do the poles. The East leans over towards the West and the circle is complete. This is the time and place, my darlings — the *only* time and the *only* place — where everybody lives happily ever after. Look!"

The Sleeping Beauty waved her hand.

Jane and Michael, glancing past it, saw three Bears hopping clumsily round a little bright-haired girl.

"Goldilocks," explained the Sleeping Beauty. "As safe and sound as you are. Oh, good-evening, Punch! How's the baby, Judy?"

She waved to a pair of long-nosed puppets who were strolling arm in arm. "They're a loving couple tonight, you see, because they're inside the Crack. Oh, look!"

This time she pointed to a towering figure. His great feet stamped upon the lawn and his head was as high as the tallest tree. A huge club was balanced on one shoulder; and perched on the other sat a laughing boy who was tweaking the big man's ear.

"That's Jack-the-Giant-Killer with his Giant. The two are bosom friends tonight." The Sleeping Beauty glanced up, smiling. "And here, at last, come the Witches!"

There was a whirr above the children's heads as a group of beady-eyed old women swooped through the air on broomsticks. A cry of welcome rose to greet them as they plunged into the crowd. Everyone rushed to shake their hands and the old women cackled with witch-like laughter.

"Nobody's frightened of them tonight. They're happy ever after!" The Sleeping Beauty's drowsy voice was like a lullaby. She stretched her arms about the children and the three stood watching the thronging figures. A Hare and a Tortoise danced by together, the Queen and the Knave of Hearts embraced, and Beauty gave her hand to the Beast. The lawns bent under the tripping feet and the air was dizzy

Jack-the-Giant-Killer with his Giant

with nodding heads as Kings and Princesses, Heroes and Witches saluted each other in the Crack between the years.

"Gangway! Gangway! Let me pass!" cried a high, clear voice.

And far away at the end of the lawn they saw the Golden Pig. He plunged through the crowd on his stiff hind legs, dividing it to left and right with a wave of his golden trotter.

"Make way! Make way!" he shouted importantly. And the crowd parted and drew aside so that it formed a double row of bowing, curtsying creatures.

For now there appeared, at the heels of the Pig, a figure that was curiously familiar. A hat with a bow was upon its head and its coat shone brightly with silver buttons. Its eyes were as blue as Willow-Pattern and its nose turned up in an airy way like the nose of a Dutch Doll.

Lightly she tripped along the path, with the Golden Pig prancing neatly before her. And as she came a cry of greeting rose up from every throat. Hats and caps and crowns and coronets were tossed into the air. And the moon itself seemed to shine more brightly as she walked beneath its rays.

"But why is *she* here?" demanded Jane, as she watched that shape come down the clearing. "Mary Poppins is not a fairy-tale."

"She's even better!" said Alfred loyally. "She's a fairy-tale come true. Besides," he rumbled, "she's the Guest of the Evening! It was she who left the books open."

Amid the happy shouts of welcome, Mary Poppins bowed to right and left. Then she marched to the centre of the lawn and, opening her black hand-bag, she took out a concertina.

"Choose your partners!" cried the Golden Pig, as he drew a flute from a pocket in his skin and put it to his mouth.

At that command, every creature there turned swiftly to his neighbour. Then the flute broke into a swinging tune; the concertina and the Four-and-Twenty Blackbirds took up the gay refrain; and a white Cat played the chorus sweetly on a hey-diddle Fiddle.

"Can it be *my* cat?" Michael wondered, as he looked for the pattern of flowers and leaves. He had no time to decide, however, for his attention was attracted by Alfred.

The grey-flannel Elephant lumbered past, uttering happy jungle cries and using his trunk as a trumpet.

"May I have the Pleasure, my dear young Lady?" He bowed to the Sleeping Beauty. She gave him her hand and they danced away, Alfred taking care not to tread on her toes and the Sleeping Beauty yawning daintily and looking very dreamy.

Everyone seemed to be choosing a partner or finding a friend in the throng.

"Kiss *me!* Kiss *me!*" cried a group of girls, as they twined their arms round a large fat schoolboy.

"Out of my way, young Georgie Porgie!" cried the Farmer's Wife, dancing with Three Blind Mice.

"Choose your partners!" cried the Golden Pig

And the fat boy plunged off into the crowd with the girls all laughing about him.

"One and two and hop and turn — that's the way it goes." Red Riding Hood, holding the Wolf by the paw, was teaching him how to dance. The Wolf, looking very humble and shy, was watching his feet as she counted.

Jane and Michael could hardly believe their eyes. But before they had time to think about it, a friendly voice hailed them.

"Do you dance?" said Robinson Crusoe gaily, as he took Jane's hand and whirled her away. She swung around, pressed to his goatskin coat, as Michael pranced off in the arms of Man Friday.

"Who is that?" asked Jane as they danced along. For there was the Blue Duck waddling past, clasped to the bosom of a large grey bird.

"That's Goosey Gander!" said Robinson Crusoe. "And there is Pinnie — with Cinderella."

She glanced round quickly. And there, sure enough, was old rag Pinnie, looking very important and proud of himself as he danced with a beautiful Lady.

Everybody had a partner. No one was lonely or left out. All the fairy-tales ever told were gathered together on that square of grass, embracing each other with joy.

"Are you happy, Jane?" Michael called to her, as he and Friday went galloping past.

"For ever and ever!" she answered smiling, and for that moment knew it was true.

The music was swifter now and wilder. It tossed among the tossing trees, it echoed above the strokes of the clock. Mary Poppins, the Pig and the Fiddling Cat were bending and swaying as they played. Again and again the Blackbirds sang and never seemed to grow weary. The fairy-tale figures swung about the children; and in their ears the fairy-tale voices were sweetly singing and laughing.

"Happy ever after!" came the echoing cry, from everyone in the Park.

"What was that?" cried Jane to her partner. For behind the shouting and the music, she had heard the boom of the clock.

"Time's nearly up!" said Robinson Crusoe. "That must have been the Sixth Stroke!"

They paused for a moment in their dance and listened to the clock.

Seven! Above the sound rose the fairy-tale music, rocking them all in its golden net.

Eight! said the steady, distant boom. And the dancing feet seemed to move more swiftly.

Nine! The trees themselves were dancing now, bending their boughs to the fairy tune.

Ten! O Lion and Unicorn, Wolf and Lamb! Friend and Enemy! Dark and Light!

Eleven! O fleeting moment! O time on the wing! How short is the space between the years! Let us be happy— happy ever after!

Twelve!

Solemn and deep the last stroke struck.

"Twelve!" The cry went up from every throat and the ring immediately broke and scattered. Bright shapes brushed swiftly past the children, Jack and his Giant, Punch and Judy. Away sped the Spider with Miss Muffett; and Humpty-Dumpty on his spindly legs. The Lion, the Unicorn, Goldilocks, Red Riding Hood and Three Blind

Mice — they streamed away across the grass and seemed to melt in the moonshine.

Cinderella and the Witches vanished. The Sleeping Beauty and the Cat with the Fiddle fled, and were lost in light. And Jane and Michael, looking round for their partners, found that Robinson Crusoe and his Man Friday had dissolved into the air.

The fairy-tale music died away, it was lost in the lordly peal of bells. For now from every tower and steeple the chimes rang out, triumphant. Big Ben, St. Paul's, St. Bride's, Old Bailey, Southwark, St. Martin's, Westminster, Bow.

But one bell sounded above the others, merry and clear and insistent.

Ting-aling-aling-aling! It was different, somehow, from the New Year bells, familiar and friendly and nearer home.

Ting-aling-aling! it cried. And mixed with its echoes was a well-known voice.

"Who wants crumpets?" the voice said loudly, demanding immediate answer.

Jane and Michael opened their eyes. They sat up and stared about them. They were in their beds, under the eiderdowns, and John and Barbara were asleep beside them. The fire glowed gaily in the grate. The morning light streamed through the Nursery window. Ting-aling! From somewhere down below in the Lane came the sound of the tinkling bell.

"I said 'Who wants crumpets?' Didn't you hear me? The Crumpet Man's down in the Lane."

There was no mistaking it. The voice was the voice of
Mary Poppins, and it sounded very impatient.

"I do!" said Michael, hurriedly.

"I do!" echoed Jane.

Mary Poppins sniffed. "Then why not say so at once!"
she said snappily. She crossed to the window and waved
her hand to summon the Crumpet Man.

Downstairs the front gate opened quickly with its usual
noisy squeak. The Crumpet Man ran up the path and knocked
at the Back Door. He was sure of an order from Number
Seventeen for all the Banks family were partial to crumpets.

Mary Poppins turned away from the window and put a
log on the fire.

Michael gazed at her sleepily for a moment. Then he
rubbed his eyes and, with a start, he woke up completely.

"I say!" he shouted. "I want my Pig! Where is it, Mary
Poppins?"

"Yes!" joined in Jane. "And I want Alfred! And where
are the Blue Duck and Pinnie?"

"On the top of the cupboard. Where else would they
be?" said Mary Poppins crossly.

They glanced up. There were the four toys standing
in a row, exactly as she had left them. And in front of
them lay *Robinson Crusoe, The Green Fairy Book* and
Mother Goose Nursery Rhymes. But the books were no
longer open as they had been last night. They were piled
upon one another neatly and all were firmly closed.

"But — how did they get back from the Park?" said Michael, very surprised.

"And where is the Pig's flute?" Jane exclaimed. "And your concertina!"

It was now Mary Poppins' turn to stare.

"My — what?" she enquired, with an ominous look.

"Your concertina, Mary Poppins! You played it last night in the Park!"

Mary Poppins turned from the fire and came towards Jane, glaring.

"I'd like you to repeat that, please!" Her voice was quiet but dreadful. "Did I understand you to say, Jane Banks, that I was in the Park last night, playing a musical instrument? Me?"

"But you were!" protested Michael bravely. "We were all there. You and the Toys and Jane and I. We were dancing with the Fairy-tales inside the Crack!"

Mary Poppins stared at them as though her ears had betrayed her. The look on her face was Simply Frightful.

"Fairy-tales inside the Crack? Humph! *You'll* have Fairy-tales inside the Bath-room, if I hear One More Word. *And* the door locked, I promise you! Crack, indeed! Cracked, more likely!"

And turning away disgustedly, she opened the door with an angry fling and hurried down the stairs.

Michael was silent for a minute, thinking and remembering.

"It's funny," he said presently. "I thought it was true. But I must have dreamed it."

Jane did not answer.

She had suddenly darted out of bed and was putting a chair against the toy-cupboard. She climbed up quickly and seized the animals and ran across to Michael.

"Feel their feet!" she whispered excitedly.

He ran his hand over the Pig's trotters; he felt the grey-flannel hooves of Alfred, the Duck's webbed feet and Pinnie's paws.

"They're wet!" he said, with astonishment.

Jane nodded.

"And look!" she cried, snatching their slippers from under the beds and Mary Poppins' shoes from the boot-box.

The slippers were drenched and stained with dew; and on the soles of Mary Poppins' shoes were wet little broken blades of grass, the sort of thing you would expect to find on shoes that have danced at night in the Park.

Michael looked up at Jane and laughed.

"It wasn't a dream, then!" he said happily.

Jane shook her head, smiling.

They sat together on Michael's bed, nodding knowingly at each other, saying in silence the secret things that could not be put into words.

Presently Mary Poppins came in with the crumpets in her hand.

They looked at her over the shoes and slippers.

She looked at them over the plate of crumpets.

A long, long look of understanding passed between the three of them. They knew that she knew that they knew.

"Is today the New Year, Mary Poppins?" asked Michael.

"Yes," she said calmly, as she put the plate down on the table.

Michael looked at her solemnly. He was thinking about the Crack.

"Shall we, too, Mary Poppins?" he asked, blurting out the question.

"Shall you, too, what?" she enquired with a sniff.

"Live happily ever afterwards?" he said eagerly.

A smile, half sad, half tender, played faintly round her mouth.

"Perhaps," she said, thoughtfully. "It all depends."

"What on, Mary Poppins?"

"On you," she said, quietly, as she carried the crumpets to the fire. . . .

CHAPTER EIGHT
The Other Door

It was a Round-the-Mulberry-Bush sort of morning, cold and rather frosty. The pale grey daylight crept through the Cherry-Trees and lapped like water over the houses. A little wind moaned through the gardens. It darted across the Park with a whistle and whined along the Lane.

"Brrrrr!" said Number Seventeen. "What can that wretched wind be doing — howling and fretting around like a ghost! Hi! Stop that, can't you? You're making me shiver!"

"Whe-ew! Whe — ew! What shall I do?" cried the wind, taking no notice.

A raking noise came from inside the house. Robertson Ay was removing the ashes and laying fresh wood in the fireplaces.

"Ah, *that's* what I need!" said Number Seventeen, as Mary Poppins lit a fire in the Nursery. "Something to warm my chilly old bones. There goes that mournful wind again! I wish it would howl somewhere else!"

"Whe — ee! Whe — ee! When will it be?" sobbed the wind among the Cherry-Trees.

The Nursery fire sprang up with a crackle. Behind their bars the bright flames danced and shone on the window-pane. Robertson Ay slouched down to the broom cupboard to take a rest from his morning labours. Mary Poppins bustled about, as usual, airing the clothes and preparing the breakfast.

Jane had wakened before anyone else, for the howl of the wind had disturbed her. And now she sat on the window-seat, sniffing the delicious scent of toast and watching her reflection in the window. Half of the Nursery shone in the garden, a room made entirely of light. The flames of the fire were warm on her back but another fire leapt and glowed before her. It danced in the air between the houses be-neath the reflection of the mantelpiece. Out there another rocking-horse was tossing his dappled head; and from the other side of the window another Jane watched and nod-ded and smiled. When Jane breathed on the window-pane and drew a face in the misty circle, her reflection did the very same thing. And all the time she was breathing and drawing, she could see right through herself. Behind the face that smiled at her were the bare black boughs of the Cherry-Trees, and right through the middle of her body was the wall of Miss Lark's house.

Presently the front door banged and Mr. Banks went away to the City. Mrs. Banks hurried into the drawing-

room to answer the morning's letters. Down in the kitch-
en Mrs. Brill was having a kipper for breakfast. Ellen had
caught another cold and was busily blowing her nose. And
up in the Nursery the fire went pop! and Mary Poppins'
apron went crackle! Altogether, except for the wind outside, it was a peaceful morning.

Not for very long, however. For Michael burst in with
a sudden rush and stood in the doorway in his pajamas.
His eyes had a silver, sleepy look as he stood there staring at Mary Poppins. He stared at her face and he stared
at her feet with an earnest, measuring, searching gaze that
missed out no part of her. Then he said "Oh!" in a disappointed voice and rubbed the sleep from his eyes.

"Well? What's the matter with *you*?" she enquired. "Lost
sixpence and found a penny?"

He shook his head dejectedly. "I dreamed you had
turned into a beautiful princess. And here you are just the
same as ever!"

She bridled and gave her head a toss. "Handsome is as
Handsome does!" she said with a haughty sniff. "I'm perfectly well as I am, thank you! *I'm* satisfied, if you're not."

He flew to her side and tried to appease her.

"Oh, I *am* satisfied, Mary Poppins!" he said eagerly.
"I just thought that if the dream had come true it would
be — er — a sort of a change."

"Change!" she exclaimed with another sniff. "You'll get

all the changes you want soon enough — I promise you, Michael Banks!"

He looked at her uneasily. What did she mean by that, he wondered.

"I was only joking, Mary Poppins. I don't want any changes, really! I only want you — for always!"

And suddenly it seemed to him that princesses were very silly creatures with nothing to be said in their favour.

"Humph!" said Mary Poppins crossly, as she planked the toast on the table. "You can't have *anything* for always — and don't you think it, sir!"

"Except you!" he retorted confidently, smiling his mischievous smile.

A strange expression came over her face. But Michael did not notice it. Out of the corner of his eye he had seen what Jane was doing. And now he was climbing up beside her to breathe on another patch of window.

"Look!" he said proudly. "I'm drawing a ship. And there's another Michael outside drawing one igzactly like it!"

"Um-hum!" said Jane, without looking up, as she gazed at her own reflection. Then suddenly she turned away and called to Mary Poppins.

"Which is the real me, Mary Poppins? The one in here or the one out there?"

With a bowl of porridge in her hand, Mary Poppins came and stood between them. Each time she breathed, her apron crackled, and the steam from the bowl went up with a puff. In silence she looked at her own reflection and smiled a satisfied smile.

Then: "—— Is this a riddle?" she demanded, sniffing.

"No, Mary Poppins," Jane said eagerly. "It's something I want to know."

For a moment they thought, as they looked at her, that she might be going to tell them. Then, apparently, she thought better of it, for she gave her head a scornful toss and turned away to the table.

"I don't know about *you*," she said, conceitedly, "but I'm glad to say that *I'm* real *wherever* I happen to be! Dress yourself, Michael, if you please! And Jane, you come to breakfast!"

Under the gleam of those steely eyes they hurried to obey her. And by the time breakfast was over and they were sitting on the floor building a Castle out of rubber bricks, they had quite forgotten their reflections. Indeed, had they looked, they would not have found them, for the fire had settled to a rosy glow and the bright flames had gone.

"That's better!" said Number Seventeen, snuggling closer into the earth.

The warmth from the fire crept through its bones and the house came alive as Mary Poppins went scuttling about it.

Today she seemed even busier than usual. She sorted

the clothes and tidied the drawers, sewed on odd buttons and mended socks. She put fresh papers on the shelves; let down the hems of Jane's and Barbara's frocks; and stitched new elastics into John's hat and Michael's. She collected Annabel's old clothes and made them into a bundle for Mrs. Brill's niece's baby. She cleaned out cupboards, sorted the toys and put the books straight in the bookcases.

"How busy she is! It makes me quite giddy!" said Michael in a whisper.

But Jane said nothing. She gazed at the crackly, bustling figure. And a thought that she could not quite get hold of was wandering round in her mind. Something — was it a memory? — whispered a word that she couldn't quite catch.

And all through the morning, the Starling sat on the Next Door chimney and screeched his endless song. Every now and then he would dart across the garden and peer through the window at Mary Poppins with bright anxious eyes. And the wind went round and round the house, sighing and crying.

The hours went by and lunch time came. And still Mary Poppins went on bustling like a very tidy tornado. She put fresh daffodils in the jam-jar; she straightened the furniture and shook out the curtains. The children felt the Nursery tremble beneath her ministering hand.

"Will she *never* stop!" Michael complained to Jane, as he added a room to the Castle.

And at that moment, as though Mary Poppins had heard what he said, she suddenly stood still.

"There!" she exclaimed, as she looked at her handiwork. "It's as Neat as a Pin. And I hope it remains so!"

Then she took down her best blue coat and brushed it. She breathed on the buttons to make them shine and pinned the starfish brooch on her collar. She tweaked and pulled at her black straw hat till the daisies stood up as stiff as soldiers. Then she took off her white crackling apron and buckled the snake-skin belt round her waist. The message written on it was clearly visible: "A Present from the Zoo."

"You haven't worn that for a long, long time," said Michael, watching with interest.

"I keep it for Best," she replied calmly, as she twitched the belt into place.

Then she took her umbrella from the corner and polished the parrot-head with bees' wax. And after that, with a quiet smile, she plucked the Tape Measure from the mantelpiece and popped it into the pocket of her coat.

Jane lifted her head quickly. Somehow, the sight of that bulging pocket made her feel strangely anxious.

"Why don't you leave the Tape Measure there? It's perfectly safe, Mary Poppins."

There was a pause. Mary Poppins appeared to be considering the question.

"I have my reasons," she said at last, as she gave a superior sniff.

"But it's always been on the mantelpiece, ever since you came back!"

"That doesn't mean that it always will be. What's good for Monday won't do for Friday," she replied with her priggish smile.

Jane turned away. What was the matter with her heart? It suddenly felt too big for her chest.

"I'm lonely," she said in a whisper to Michael, taking care not to look at him.

"You can't be lonely as long as I'm here!" he put his last brick on the roof of the Castle.

"It's not that kind of loneliness. I feel I'm going to lose something."

"Perhaps it's your tooth," he said, with interest. "Try it and see if it wobbles."

Jane shook her head quickly. Whatever it was she was going to lose, she knew it was not a tooth.

"Oh, for just one more brick!" sighed Michael. "Everything's done but the chimney!"

Mary Poppins came swiftly across the room.

"There you are! That's what it needs!" she said. And she stooped and put one of her own dominoes in the place where the chimney should be.

"Hooray! It's completely finished!" he cried, glancing up at her with delight. Then he saw that she had placed the box of dominoes beside him. The sight of them made him queerly uneasy.

"You mean —— " he said, swallowing. "You mean — we may keep them?"

He had always wanted those dominoes. But never before had Mary Poppins allowed him to touch her possessions. What did it mean? It was so unlike her. And suddenly, as she nodded at him, he, too, felt a pang of loneliness.

"Oh!" he broke out, with an anxious wail. "What's wrong, Mary Poppins? What can be the matter?"

"Wrong!" Her eyes snapped angrily. "I give you a nice respectable present and that's all the thanks I get! What's wrong indeed! I'll know better next time."

He rushed at her wildly and clutched her hand. "Oh, I didn't mean that, Mary Poppins! I — thank you. It was just a sudden idea I had —— "

"Those ideas are going to get you into trouble one of these fine bright days. You mark my words!" she snorted. "Now, get your hats, please, all of you! We'll go for a walk to the Swings."

At the sight of that familiar glare their anxiety melted away. They flew to get ready, shouting and laughing, and knocking the Castle down as they ran.

The thin Spring sun shone over the Park as they hurried across the Lane. Green smoke hung around the Cherry-Trees where the small new leaves were sprouting. The scent of primroses was in the air and the birds were rehearsing their songs for summer.

"I'll race you to the Swings!" shouted Michael.

"We'll have them all to ourselves!" cried Jane. For nobody else was in the clearing where the five swings stood and waited.

In no time they had scrambled for places and Jane and Michael, John and Barbara were each on a swing of their own. Annabel, looking like a white woollen egg, shared hers with Mary Poppins.

"Now — one, two, THREE!" cried Michael loudly, and the swings swayed from the cross-beam. Higher and higher the children swung, swooping like birds through the delicate sunlight. Up they went with their heads to the sky and down they came with their feet to the earth. The trees seemed to spread their branches below them; the roofs of the houses nodded and bowed.

"It's like flying!" Jane cried happily, as the earth turned a somersault under her feet. She glanced across at Michael. His hair was tossing in all directions as he rode through the air. The Twins were squeaking like excited mice. And beyond them, with a dignified air, Mary Poppins swung backwards and forwards. One hand held Annabel on her knee and the other grasped her umbrella. Her eyes, as she rode her flying swing, shone with a strange, bright gleam. They were bluer than Jane had ever seen them, blue with the blueness of faraway. They seemed to look past the trees and houses, and out beyond all the seas and mountains, and over the rim of the world.

The afternoon faded and the Park grew grey as it tilted

beneath their feet. But Jane and Michael took no notice. They were wrapped in a dream with Mary Poppins, a dream that swung them up and down between the earth and the sky, a rocking, riding, lulling dream that would never come to an end.

But come to an end it did, at last. The sun went over and the dream went with it. As the last rays spread across the Park, Mary Poppins put her foot to the ground and her swing stopped with a jerk.

"It is time to go," she said, quietly. And because her voice had, for once, no sternness, they stopped their swings immediately and obeyed without protesting. The perambulator gave its familiar groan as she dumped the Twins and Annabel into it. Jane and Michael walked quietly beside her. The earth was still swaying beneath their feet. They were happy and calm and silent.

Creak, creak! went the perambulator along the path.

Trip, trip, went Mary Poppins' shoes.

Michael glanced up as the last light fell on the faint green leaves of the Cherry-Trees.

"I believe," he said dreamily to Jane, "that Nellie Rubina's been here!"

"Here today and gone tomorrow — that's me!" cried a tinkling voice.

They turned to find Nellie Rubina herself rolling along on her wooden disc. And behind her came the wheeling shape of old Uncle Dodger.

"What a roll I've had!" cried Nellie Rubina. "I've looked for you everywhere!" she panted. "How are you all? Doing nicely, I hope! I wanted to see you, dear Miss Poppins, to give you a —— "

"And also," said Uncle Dodger eagerly, "to wish you a very good —— "

"Uncle Dodger!" said Nellie Rubina, with a warning glint in her eye.

"Oh, excuse me! Begging your pardon, my dear!" the old man answered quickly.

"Just a Little Something to remember us by," Nellie Rubina went on. Then, thrusting out her wooden arm, she popped a small white object into Mary Poppins' hand.

The children crowded to look at it.

"It's a Conversation!" Michael exclaimed.

Jane peered at the letters in the fading light. " 'Fare Thee Well, my Fairy Fay!' " she read out. "Are you going away, then, Nellie Rubina?"

"Oh, dear me, yes! Tonight's the night!" Nellie Rubina gave a tinkling laugh as she glanced at Mary Poppins.

"You can keep it to eat on the way, Miss Poppins!" Uncle Dodger nodded at the Conversation.

"Uncle Dodger!" cried Nellie Rubina.

"Oh, my! Oh, my! Out of turn again! I'm too old, that's what it is, my dear. And begging your pardon, of course."

"Well, it's very kind of you both, I'm sure," said Mary Poppins politely. You could see she was pleased by the way she smiled. Then she tucked the Conversation into her pocket and gave the pram a push.

"Oh, do wait a minute, Mary Poppins!" cried a breathless voice behind them. A patter of steps came along the path and the children turned quickly.

"Why, it's Mr. and Mrs. Turvy!" cried Michael, as a tall, thin shape and a round, fat one came forward, hand in hand.

"We now call ourselves the Topsy-Turvies. We think it sounds better." Mr. Turvy looked down at them over his glasses as his wife shook hands all round.

"Well, Mary," he went on, in his gloomy voice, "we thought we'd drop in, just for a moment — to say So Long, you know."

"And not *too* long, we hope, dear Mary!" added Mrs. Turvy, smiling. Her round, fat face shook like a jelly and she looked extremely happy.

"Oh, thank you kindly, Cousin Arthur! And you, too, Topsy!" said Mary Poppins, as she shook them both by the hand.

"What does it mean — So Long?" asked Jane, as she

leant against Mary Poppins. Something — perhaps it was the darkness — made her suddenly want to be very close to that warm and comforting figure.

"It means my daughters!" a small voice screeched, as a shape emerged from the shadows. "So long, so wide, so huge, so stupid — the great Gallumping Giraffes."

And there on the path stood Mrs. Corry with her coat all covered with threepenny-bits. And behind her, Fannie and Annie stalked, like a pair of mournful giants.

"Well, here we are again!" shrieked Mrs. Corry, as she grinned at the staring children. "H'm! Growing up fast, aren't they, Mary Poppins? I can see that they won't need *you* much longer!"

Mary Poppins gave a nod of agreement as Michael, with a cry of protest, rushed to her side.

"We'll always need her — always!" he cried, hugging Mary Poppins' waist so tightly that he felt her strong hard bones.

She glared at him like an angry panther.

"Kindly do not crush me, Michael! I am not a Sardine in a Tin!"

"Well, I just came to have a word with you," Mrs. Corry cackled on. "An old word, Mary, and one that is best said quickly. As I used to tell Solomon when he was making that fuss about the Queen of Sheba — if you've got to say it sometime, why not now?" Mrs. Corry looked searchingly at Mary Poppins. Then she added softly, "Good-bye, my dear!"

"Are you going away, too?" Michael demanded, as he stared at Mrs. Corry.

She gave a merry shriek of laughter. "Well — yes, I am, in a manner of speaking! Once one goes they all go — that's the way of it. Now, Fannie and Annie ——" she glanced around, "what have you idiots done with those presents?"

"Here, Mother!" the sisters answered nervously. And the huge hands dropped into Mary Poppins' palm two tiny pieces of gingerbread. One was shaped like a heart and the other like a star.

Mary Poppins gave a cry of delight.

"Why, Mrs. Corry! *What* a surprise! This is a Treat as well as a Pleasure!"

"Oh, it's nothing. Just a Souvenir." Mrs. Corry airily waved her hand, and her little elastic-sided boots danced along beside the perambulator.

"All your friends seem to be here tonight!" remarked Michael to Mary Poppins.

"Well, what do you think I am — a Hermit? I suppose I can see my friends when I like!"

"I was only remarking ——" he began, when a glad shriek interrupted him.

"Why, Albert — if it isn't you!" cried Mrs. Corry gaily. And she ran to meet a roly-poly figure that was hurrying towards them. The children gave a shout of joy as they recognized Mr. Wigg.

"Well, Bless my Boots. It's Clara Corry!" cried Mr. Wigg, shaking her hand affectionately.

"I didn't know you knew each other!" exclaimed Jane, looking very surprised.

"What *you* don't know would fill a Dictionary," Mary Poppins broke in with a snort.

"Know each other? Why, we were children together — weren't we, Albert?" cried Mrs. Corry.

Mr. Wigg chuckled. "Ah, the good old days!" he answered cheerily. "Well, how are you, Mary, my girl?"

"Nicely, thank you, Uncle Albert. Mustn't complain," replied Mary Poppins.

"I thought I'd step up for One Last Word. Pleasant trip and all that. It's a nice night for it." Mr. Wigg glanced round at the clear blue dusk that was creeping through the Park.

"A nice night for what?" demanded Michael. He hoped Mary Poppins would not be lonely with her friends going off like this. But, after all, he thought to himself — she's still got me and what more could she want?

"A nice night to go sailing — that's what it's for!" roared Admiral Boom in his rollicking voice. He was striding through the trees towards them, singing as he came:

"Sailing, sailing, over the Bounding Main,
    And many a stormy Wind shall blow

Till we come home again!
Sailing, sailing —"

"Ahoy there, lubbers! Hoist the mainsail! Up with the anchor and let her go. For away I'm bound to go — oho! — 'cross the wide Missouri!" He blew his nose with a sound like a foghorn and looked at Mary Poppins.

"All aboard?" he enquired gruffly, putting a hand on her shoulder.

"All aboard, Sir," she answered primly, and she gave him a curious look.

"Hrrrrrrrrmph! Well ——

"I'll be true to my love,
If my Love will be tru-ue to me!"

he sang, in a voice that was almost gentle. "Here ——" he broke off. "Port and Starboard! Cockles and Whelks! You can't do that to a Sailor!"

"Balloons *and* Balloons!" cried a high-pitched voice as a little shape went whizzing past and knocked off the Admiral's hat.

It was the Balloon Woman. One small balloon flew from her hand. It bounced her upon the end of its string and swept her away through the shadows.

"Good-bye *and* Good-bye, my Dearie Duck!" she called as she disappeared.

"There she goes — off like a streak of lightning!" cried Jane, gazing after her.

"Well, she's certainly not a creeping Snail, like *some* people I could mention! Kindly walk up!" said Mary Poppins. "I haven't all night to waste!"

"I should think not!" Mrs. Corry said, grinning.

They walked up. For once they were eager to do anything she told them. They put their hands on the perambulator beside her black-gloved fingers. And the blue dusk lapped them round like a river as they hurried along with the chattering group.

They were nearly at the Park Gates now. The Lane stretched darkly in front of them and from it came a strain of music. Jane and Michael looked at each other. What could it be? said their upraised brows. Then their curiosity got the better of them. They wanted to stay with Mary Poppins but they also wanted to see what was happening. They gave one glance at her dark blue figure and then began to run.

"Oh, look!" cried Jane, as she reached the Gate. "It's Mr. Twigley with a Hurdy-gurdy!"

And Mr. Twigley it was indeed, drawing a sweet wild tune from the box as he busily turned the handle. Beside him stood a small bright figure that was vaguely familiar.

"And all of them made of the Finest Sugar," it was saying gaily to Mr. Twigley as the children crossed the road. Then, of course, they knew who it was.

"Stare, stare,
Like a Bear,
Then you'll know me
Everywhere!"

chanted Miss Calico cheerfully, as she waved her hand towards them.

"Could you move your feet a bit, please, kids! You're standing on one of my roses!"

Bert, the Matchman, crouched on the pavement, right at their own front gate. He was drawing a large bouquet of flowers in coloured chalks on the asphalt. Ellen and the Policeman were watching him. And Miss Lark and her dogs were listening to the music as they stood outside Next Door.

"Wait a minute," she cried to Mr. Twigley, "while I run in and get you a shilling!"

Mr. Twigley smiled his twinkly smile and shook his head gently.

"Don't bother, ma'am," he advised Miss Lark. "A shilling would be no use to me. I'm doing it All for Love." And the children saw him lift his eyes and exchange a look with Mary Poppins as she strode out of the Park. He wound the handle with all his might and the tune grew louder and quicker.

"One Forget-me-not — and then it's finished," the Matchman murmured to himself as he added a flower to the bunch.

"That's dainty, Bert!" said Mary Poppins admiringly. She had pushed the perambulator up behind him and was gazing at the picture. He sprang to his feet with a little cry and, plucking the bouquet from the pavement, he pressed it into her hand.

"They're yours, Mary," he told her shyly. "I drew them all for you!"

"Did you really, Bert?" she said with a smile. "Well, I just don't know how to thank you!" She hid her blushing face in the flowers and the children could smell the scent of roses.

The Matchman looked at her glowing eyes and smiled a loving smile.

"It's tonight — isn't it, Mary?" he said.

"Yes, Bert," she said, nodding, as she gave him her hand. The Matchman looked at it sadly for a moment. Then he bent his head and kissed it.

"Good-bye, then, Mary!" they heard him whisper.

And she answered softly, "Good-bye, Bert!"

"What is all this about tonight?" demanded Michael, inquisitively.

"Tonight is the happiest night of my life!" said Miss Lark as she listened to the Hurdy-gurdy. "I never heard such beautiful music. It makes my feet simply twinkle!"

"Well, let 'em twinkle with mine!" roared the Admiral. And he snatched Miss Lark away from her gate and polka-ed along the Lane.

"Oh, Admiral!" they heard her cry, as he swung her round and round.

"Lovey-dovey-cat's-eyes!" cooed Mrs. Turvy. And Mr. Turvy, looking very embarrassed, allowed her to dance him round.

"Wot about it — eh?" the Policeman smirked, and before Ellen had time to blow her nose, he had whirled her into the dance.

One, two, three! One, two, three! High and sweet, the music flowed from the Hurdy-gurdy. The street lamps blazed with sudden brightness and speckled the Lane with light and shadow. One, two, three, went Miss Calico's feet, as she danced alone beside Mr. Twigley. It was such a wild and merry tune that Jane and Michael could stand still no longer. Off they darted and one, two, three, their feet went tapping on the echoing road.

"'Ere! Wot's all this? Observe the Rules! We can't 'ave dancing in Public Places! Move on, now, don't obstruct the traffic!" The Park Keeper, goggling as usual, came threading his way through the Lane.

"Mercy me and a Jumping Bean! You're just the man I want!" shrieked Miss Calico. And before the Park Keeper knew where he was, she had swung him into the mazy dance where he gulped and gaped and twirled.

"Round we go, Clara!" cried Mr. Wigg, swinging past with Mrs. Corry.

"I used to do this with Henry the Eighth — and oh, what a time we had!" she shrieked. "Get along, clumsies! Keep your feet to yourselves!" she added, in a different voice, to Fannie and Annie who were dancing together like a pair of gloomy elephants.

"I've never been so happy before!" came Miss Lark's excited cry.

"You should go to sea, my dear Lucinda! Everyone's happy at sea!" roared the Admiral, as he polka-ed madly along.

"I do believe I will," she replied.

And her two dogs looked at each other aghast and hoped she would change her mind.

Deeper and deeper grew the dusk as the dancers whirled in a ring. And there in the centre stood Mary Poppins with her flowers clasped in her hands. She rocked the perambulator gently and her foot beat time with the music. The Matchman watched her from the pavement.

Straight and stiff she stood there, smiling, and her eyes went roving from one to the other — Miss Lark and the Admiral, the Topsy-Turvies; the two Noahs rolling around on their discs; Miss Calico clutching the Park Keeper; Mrs. Corry in the arms of Mr. Wigg; and Mrs. Corry's big daughters. Then her bright glance fell on the two young children who were dancing round in the ring. She looked at them for a long, long moment, watching their bright enchanted faces and their arms going out to each other.

And suddenly, as though they felt that look upon them,

And there in the centre stood Mary Poppins

they stopped in the middle of their dance and ran to her, laughing and breathless.

"Mary Poppins!" they both cried, pressing against her. Then they found they had nothing else to say. Her name seemed to be enough.

She put her arms about their shoulders and looked into their eyes. It was a long, deep, searching look that plunged right down to their very hearts and saw what was there. Then she smiled to herself and turned away. She took her parrot-headed umbrella from the perambulator and gathered Annabel into her arms.

"I must go in now, Jane and Michael! You two can bring the Twins later."

They nodded, still panting from the dance.

"Now, be good children!" she said quietly. "And remember all I have told you."

They smiled at her reassuringly. What a funny thing to say, they thought. As if they would dare forget!

She gave the Twins' curls a gentle rumple; she buttoned up Michael's coat at the neck and straightened Jane's collar.

"Now, spit-spot and away we go!" she cried gaily to Annabel.

Then off she tripped through the garden-gate, with the baby, the flowers and the parrot umbrella held lightly in her arms. Up the steps went the prim, trim figure, walking with a jaunty air as though she was thoroughly pleased with herself.

"Farewell, Mary Poppins!" the dancers cried, as she paused at the Front Door.

She glanced back over her shoulder and nodded. Then the Hurdy-gurdy gave a loud sweet peal and the Front Door closed behind her.

Jane shivered as the music ceased. Perhaps it was the frost in the air that made her feel so lonely.

"We'll wait till all the people leave and then we'll go in," she said.

She glanced around at the group of dancers. They were standing still upon the pavement and seemed to be waiting for something. For every face was gazing upwards at Number Seventeen.

"What can they be looking at?" said Michael, as he craned his own head backwards.

Then a glow appeared at the Nursery windows and a dark shape moved across it. The children knew it was Mary Poppins, lighting the evening fire. And presently the flames sprang up. They sparkled on the window-panes and shone through the darkening garden. Higher and higher leapt the blaze, brighter and brighter the windows gleamed. Then suddenly they saw the Nursery reflected upon Miss Lark's side wall. There it gleamed, high above the garden, with its sparkling fire and the mantelpiece and the old armchair and ——

"The Door! The Door!" A breathless cry went up from the crowd in the Lane.

What door? Jane and Michael stared at each other. And suddenly — they knew!

"Oh, Michael! It isn't her friends who are going away!" cried Jane in an anguished voice. "It's — oh, hurry, hurry! We must go and find her!"

With trembling hands they hauled out the Twins and dragged them through the gate. They tore at the Front Door, rushed upstairs and burst into the Nursery.

Their faces fell as they stared at the room, for everything in it was as quiet and peaceful as it had always been. The fire was crackling behind its bars and, cosily tucked inside her cot, Annabel was softly cooing. The bricks they had used for the morning's Castle were neatly piled in a corner. And beside them lay the precious box of Mary Poppins' dominoes.

"Oh!" they panted, surprised and puzzled to find everything just the same.

Everything? No! There was one thing missing.

"The camp bed!" Michael cried. "It's gone! Then — where is Mary Poppins?"

He ran to the bathroom and out on the landing and back to the Nursery again.

"Mary Poppins! Mary Poppins! Mary Poppins!"

Then Jane glanced up from the fire to the window and gave a little cry.

"Oh, Michael, Michael! There she is! And there is the Other Door!"

Away she stalked through the Nursery's reflection

He followed the line of her pointing finger and his mouth opened wide.

For there, on the outer side of the window, another Nursery glimmered. It stretched from Number Seventeen to the wall of Miss Lark's house; and everything in the real Nursery was reflected in that shining room. There was Annabel's gleaming cot and the table made of light. There was the fire, leaping up in mid-air; and there, at last, was the Other Door, exactly the same as the one behind them. It shimmered like a panel of light at the other side of the garden. Beside it stood their own reflections and towards it, along the airy floor, tripped the figure of Mary Poppins. She carried the carpet bag in her hand; and the Matchman's flowers and the parrot umbrella were tucked beneath her arm. Away she stalked through the Nursery's reflection, away through the shimmering likenesses of the old familiar things. And as she went, the daisies nodded on the crown of her black straw hat.

A loud cry burst from Michael's mouth as he rushed towards the window.

"Mary Poppins!" he cried. "Come back! Come back!"

Behind him the Twins began to grizzle.

"Oh, please, Mary Poppins, come back to us!" called Jane, from the window-seat.

But Mary Poppins took no notice. She strode on swiftly towards the Door that shimmered in the air.

"She won't get anywhere that way!" said Michael. "It will only lead to Miss Lark's wall."

But even as he spoke, Mary Poppins reached the Other Door and pulled it wide open. A gasp of surprise went up from the children. For the wall they had expected to see had entirely disappeared. Beyond Mary Poppins' straight blue figure there was nothing but field on field of sky, and the dark spreading night.

"Come back, Mary Poppins!" they cried together, in a last despairing wail.

And as though she had heard them, she paused for a minute, with one foot on the threshold. The starfish sparkled on her collar as she glanced back swiftly towards the Nursery. She smiled at the four sad watching faces and waved her bouquet of flowers. Then she snapped the parrot umbrella open and stepped out into the night.

The umbrella wobbled for a moment and the light from the fire shone full upon it as it swayed in the air. Then, with a bound, as though glad to be free, it soared away through the sky. Up, up went Mary Poppins with it, tightly holding the parrot handle as she cleared the tops of the trees. And as she went, the Hurdy-gurdy broke out with a peal of music, as loud and proud and triumphant as any wedding march.

Back in the Nursery the great blaze faded and sank into crimson coals. The flames went down and with them went the shining other room. Soon there was nothing to be seen but the Cherry-Trees waving through the air and the blank brick wall of Miss Lark's house.

But above the roof a bright form rose, flying higher every minute. It seemed to have gathered into itself the sparkle and flame of the fire. For it glowed like a little core of light in the black frosty sky.

Leaning upon the window-seat, the four children watched it. Their cheeks lay heavily in their hands and their hearts were heavy within their breasts. They did not try to explain it to themselves, for they knew there were things about Mary Poppins that could never be explained. Where she had come from nobody knew, and where she was going they could not guess. They were certain only of one thing — that she had kept her promise. She had stayed with them till the Door opened and then she had left them. And they could not tell if they would ever see that trim shape again.

Michael reached out for the box of dominoes. He put it on the sill beside Jane. And together they held it as they watched the umbrella go sailing through the sky.

Presently Mrs. Banks came in.

"What — sitting all alone, my darlings?" she cried as she snapped on the light. "Where's Mary Poppins?" she enquired, with a glance round the room.

"Gone, ma'am," said a resentful voice, as Mrs. Brill appeared on the landing.

Mrs. Banks' face had a startled look.

"What do you mean?" she demanded anxiously.

"Well, it's this way," Mrs. Brill replied. "I was listenin'

to a Nurdy-gurdy that's down in the Lane, when I sees the
empty perambulator and the Match-man wheelin' it up to
the door. "'Ullo!' I says, 'where's that Mary Poppins?' And
'e tells me she's gone again. Lock, stock and barrer gone.
Not even a note on 'er pincushion!"

"Oh, what shall I do?" wailed Mrs. Banks, sitting down
on the old armchair.

"Do? You can come and dance with me!" cried Mr.
Banks' voice, as he raced upstairs.

"Oh, don't be so silly, George! Something's happened. Mary Poppins has gone again!" Mrs. Banks' face was a tragedy. "George! George! Please listen to me!" she begged.

For Mr. Banks had taken no notice. He was waltzing round and round the room, holding out his coattails.

"I can't! There's a Hurdy-gurdy down in the Lane and it's playing the *Blue Danube*. Ta-rum pom-pom-pom — de-di, de-dum!"

And, pulling Mrs. Banks from the chair, he waltzed her round, singing lustily. Then they both collapsed on the window-seat among the watching children.

"But, George — this is serious!" Mrs. Banks protested, half-laughing, half-crying, as she pinned up her hair.

"I see something much more serious!" he exclaimed, as he glanced through the Nursery window. "A shooting star! Look at it! Wish on it, children!"

Away through the sky streaked the shining spark, cleaving a path through the darkness. And as they watched it, every heart was filled with sudden sweetness. Down in the Lane the music ceased and the dancers stood gazing, hand in hand.

"My dear Love!" Mr. Banks said tenderly, as he touched Mrs. Banks' cheek. And they put their arms around each other and wished on the star.

Jane and Michael held their breath as the sweetness brimmed up within them. And the thing they wished was that all their lives they might remember Mary Poppins.

Where and How and When and Why — had nothing to do with them. They knew that as far as she was concerned those questions had no answers. The bright shape speeding through the air above them would forever keep its secret. But in the summer days to come and the long nights of winter, they would remember Mary Poppins and think of all she had told them. The rain and the sun would remind them of her, and the birds and the beasts and the changing seasons. Mary Poppins herself had flown away, but the gifts she had brought would remain for always.

"We'll never forget you, Mary Poppins!" they breathed, looking up at the sky.

Her bright shape paused in its flight for a moment and gave an answering wave. Then darkness folded its wing about her and hid her from their eyes.

"It's gone!" said Mr. Banks, with a sigh, looking out at the starless night.

Then he pulled the curtains across the window and drew them all to the fire. . . .

Sussex, England,
New York, U.S.A.

GLORIA IN EXCELSIS DEO

P. L. TRAVERS (1899–1996) was a drama critic, travel essayist, reviewer, lecturer, and the creator of Mary Poppins. Travers wrote eight Mary Poppins books altogether, including *Mary Poppins* (1934), *Mary Poppins Comes Back* (1935), *Mary Poppins Opens the Door* (1943), and *Mary Poppins in the Park* (1952). Ms. Travers wrote several other children's books as well as adult books, but it is for the character of Mary Poppins that she is best remembered.